D0041263

The LION of MARS

More Novels by Jennifer L. Holm

The Fourteenth Goldfish

The Third Mushroom

Full of Beans

Turtle in Paradise

Middle School Is Worse Than Meatloaf

Eighth Grade Is Making Me Sick

Penny from Heaven

The Boston Jane series

The May Amelia books

By Jennifer L. Holm and Matthew Holm

The Evil Princess vs. the Brave Knight

Babymouse: Tales from the Locker

The Babymouse series

The Squish series

The Sunny series

My First Comics series

The Comics Squad series (with Jarrett J. Krosoczka)

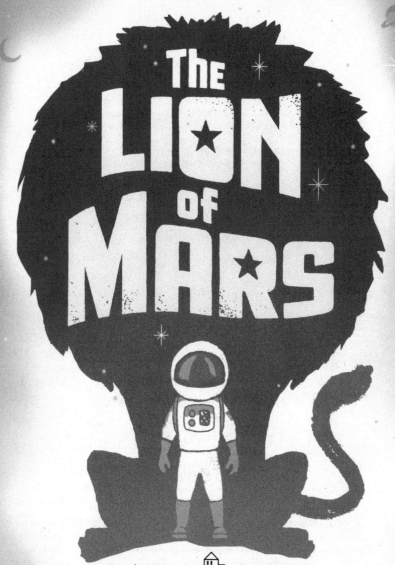

JENNIFER L. HOLM

The LION of MARS

Random House New York

All rights reserved. Published in the United States by Random House Children's Books,
a division of Penguin Random House LLC, New York.

Random House and the colophon are registered trademarks of
Penguin Random House LLC.

Photograph credits: pp. 253, 256 courtesy Jennifer L. Holm;
p. 255 courtesy NASA/JPL/Cornell University

Visit us on the Web! rhcbooks.com

Educators and librarians, for a variety of teaching tools, visit us at
RHTeachersLibrarians.com

Library of Congress Cataloging-in-Publication Data is available upon request.
ISBN 978-0-593-12181-8 (hc)—ISBN 978-0-593-12182-5 (lib. bdg.)—
ISBN 978-0-593-37694-2 (int'l ed.)—ISBN 978-0-593-12183-2 (ebook)

The text of this book is set in 12-point Bell MT Pro.
Interior design by Cathy Bobak

Printed in the United States of America
10 9 8 7 6 5 4 3 2 1
First Edition

To my cat-loving son
and his sister, whose first word was "rock."
And, of course, to my husband,
who applied to be an astronaut.
See you on Mars.

CONTENTS

DATE: 3.5.2091
FROM: CDR Dexter
TO: US Terrestrial Command
MESSAGE: Situation Report

The surface digi-cam at the northwest quadrant of the settlement has been destroyed. The pole supporting it was knocked over as well. It is my conclusion that this was done deliberately by a hostile actor.

Please advise.

Sai Dexter, COMMANDER
Expeditionary & Settlement Team
United States Territory, Mars

Chapter One

NEST

The trip to Mars was the hardest thing they'd ever experienced. That's what the grown-ups said. The small, cramped ship. The constant fear of something going wrong. The knowledge that they could never return to Earth.

But honestly, it sounded like a cakewalk compared to sharing a bedroom with Albie.

Because he snored.

I hadn't had a decent night's sleep since Albie started bunking with me. I'd tried just about everything to block the noise: earplugs, sleeping under the blanket, even a thick hat with earflaps. But none of them worked.

It was surprising because Albie was perfect. He was easygoing and did his chores without complaining. Of all us kids, he was the least likely to throw a fuss. The grown-ups trusted him, even Sai. But it turned out there was one thing Albie *wasn't* good at: sleeping quietly. And I didn't know which was worse: Albie's snoring or Trey wanting to change rooms.

For as long as I could remember, Trey had slept in the bed across from mine. My drawings of cats and his drawings of aliens had papered the walls. Our plastic models crowded the shelves together. Then, two months ago, Trey suddenly asked to switch bedrooms. Next thing I knew, Trey was sleeping across the hall in the older kids' room with Vera and Flossy, while Albie was snoring in mine.

And me?

I wasn't sleeping at all.

Neither was Leo, from the looks of it. The old cat was sitting up in bed, flicking his tail in annoyance.

This room-switching thing had happened once before. Back when Trey and I were little, the grown-ups had moved us boys into one room and the girls into the other. Albie was older than me and Trey and so he was allowed to stay up later. The problem was that Albie would make a lot of noise when he came to bed, and he'd wake us up. The experiment was abandoned after a week. Now, all these years later, Albie was keeping me awake again.

Across the room from me, Albie let out a loud, waffling snort. I groaned, pulling the pillow over my head.

"Albie," I said.

He didn't move.

"Albie!" I shouted.

He sat up abruptly, looking around the dimly lit room

in confusion. Albie was tall, with broad shoulders. Darby said he would've made a good football player. Football was an Earth game where you threw around a ball and knocked into people. I didn't really understand it.

"What's wrong, Bell?" Albie asked, his hair sticking out crazily everywhere. It was always funny to see him without his Dodgers ball cap. He only took it off at bedtime.

"You're snoring!" I said.

"Oh," he said. "I thought there was an emergency."

"It *is* an emergency! I can't sleep!"

"I'm so sorry, Bell," he mumbled, and lay back down. "I promise not to snore anymore."

It was hard to be angry at Albie. He was kind and gentle—a big teddy bear when it came right down to it.

A big *snoring* teddy bear.

"Aw, dust it," I muttered. Albie could have the room to himself. I grabbed my blanket and left, Leo padding after me.

Not that I blamed him.

Even a cat couldn't take Albie's snoring.

Leo and I walked down the twisting corridor, our way lit by the cool blue light of nighttime. The light changed to mirror the time of day. In the morning, the blue would transform to a warm, bright yellow. This was supposed to help us have a sense of time because the settlement was mostly underground. It had been built in a giant lava tube—a massive, cavelike space left behind by flowing lava millions of years ago. It was the perfect prebuilt habitat, keeping us safe from the surface dangers of Mars—radiation, extreme freezing temperatures, and dust.

The interior walls were constructed from a space-tech gray rubber that curved gently, flowing from one room to the next like a smile. The rooms were round, almost bubble-like, for improved structural integrity. Sai told me he'd thrown out the old rules when he designed the settlement. Apparently, on Earth, people lived in boxy structures with hard corners.

Earth sounded sharp to me.

This corridor was a history of my childhood. There was the spot where I banged into the wall with my scooter. The scratches on the ceiling from when I'd tried to make my toy spaceship fly. (It didn't work.) And, of course, the ruler on the wall where Meems recorded our growth with a thick black pen. She joked that as some of the first human children to grow up on Mars, we were a living experiment.

Farther down the way was a board with digi-pics of us when we'd arrived on Mars. We were much older now than the babies on the wall. Albie was seventeen, the oldest in Earth years. Then came Flossy (sixteen), Vera (fifteen), Trey (fourteen), and me (eleven).

I might have been the youngest, but at least I still knew how to have fun. Unlike the older kids, who'd become moody grumps when they turned thirteen.

Of course, in Mars years we were much younger. It takes Mars 687 days to go around the sun, so a "Mars year" is 687 days, which meant I was only five and Trey was seven.

Ahead of me, Leo stopped to sniff at something, his tail flicking in the air. When I was little, there had been a lot of cats. Bella. Mochi. Harley. Sesame. Little Cat. As the years went by, the cats died, and Leo was the only one left. But I still remembered them all.

Then Leo and I were leaving the children's wing and passing the shared areas—the recreation room and the mess hall and kitchen—that bookended the two sleeping wings. The recreation room was illuminated by the flickering light of a digi-reel that someone had left playing.

Like the rest of the settlement, the room was painted a pale blue. It was supposed to be a soothing color that mimicked the Earth sky. There was an L-shaped couch with a loop rug woven from old clothing. Darby had created the rocking chair from plastic barrels. Everything was recycled on Mars. Even the plant that decorated the room was made from algae paper, although it was getting old and the leaves had become brittle and started to crumble.

Aside from the couch and rocking chair, there was the small plastic table we had played at when we were little. These days, it held Flossy's sewing machine and fabric instead of our clay and crayons. Then there was the plastic display case next to the wall, which housed the rocks we children had collected over the years.

After that was the mess hall. It smelled like tonight's supper: an algae casserole that was one of Salty Bill's standard meals. No one was around, so I made a quick stop in the kitchen and grabbed a few ginger cookies. Salty Bill didn't like anyone taking food when he wasn't there, but I figured he wouldn't miss them.

Then I was in the grown-ups' wing. First was Meems's room. I could find my way to it with my eyes closed; when we woke up sick at night, she was the one we went to. Past it was Salty Bill's room. Across from it was Phinneus's room. As I passed Eliana and Darby's room, I could hear soft snoring. Eliana had always complained about her husband's snoring, but I never understood what she was talking about. I sure did now.

Everyone's rooms were dark except for Sai's. There was light under his door, and I wondered what kept him from sleep. I left the living quarters behind and followed the corridor that led to the work areas. This part of the settlement was usually buzzing with activity during the day. But in the middle of the night, the only sound was from the air scrubbers humming softly in the background like a lullaby. I passed the exercise room, Sai's workshop, the sick bay, various workrooms, the generator room, and, my favorite, the algae farm.

Just past the algae farm was a circular staircase. I climbed up and up and up the bouncing plastic stairs. I was a little out of breath when I finally reached the communications and observations rooms, also known as COR. It was aboveground and where we sent and received messages from Earth. The grown-ups jokingly called it the Phone Booth. The COR was the crew's original habitat when they'd first arrived on Mars. Installed by robots, it was a simple domelike structure. There was a wide window with a sweeping view of the dusty red Martian landscape. No one spent much time here except for Sai. As commander, he sent situation reports to Earth Command. Also, he could monitor the weather better up here. It was the perfect spot to watch whirling dust devils.

I liked the echoes of the room's previous life. Taped on the walls were colorful maps of Earth places. Pennsylvania. Alabama. Alaska. Michigan. It had been tradition for the crew to bring a map from their home state.

Then there were the plastic lockers for the crew members' belongings. They'd decorated them with stickers and pictures. The front of Sai's locker had a list of all the places he'd visited.

BUCKET LIST

~~Everest~~
~~Antarctica~~
Moon
Mars

Best of all, it was quiet up here. I settled on the couch under the blanket and munched on the cookies. Outside the wide window, Phobos, one of our two moons, was a glowing lump in the darkness. Above it was Earth, a bright, shining star.

I wondered if the people on Earth thought about us as much as we did about them. Even though I'd seen lots of digi-pics, I still had a hard time imagining Earth. The pool of endless water called the ocean. The places with trees called forests. And, of course, the animals. Phinneus had told me about the birds that flew through the sky and made their homes, called nests, in trees high above the ground.

As I closed my eyes with Leo curled at my feet, I felt like a bird in a quiet, safe nest—my home.

One that I never, ever wanted to leave.

Chapter Two

A GOOD DAY

I blinked my eyes open. The dome was bathed in warm pink light.

It was morning.

And there was something heavy on my chest.

"Meow!"

That something was Leo. He was sitting on me.

"Meeee-ow!" he said again, more loudly. I understood a little Cat, and that meant *I'm hungry!*

"I guess you want breakfast," I said.

Satisfied that I was finally awake, he leapt off me with a swish of his tail, landing with a soft thud on the floor.

I stood up and yawned, walking over to the window. The landscape stretched out in varying shades of dusty red as far as I could see. The low-hanging sun was a small dot against a pink sky with wispy blue clouds.

Sunrise on Mars was magical.

Just beyond the window was our backyard. The swooping craters where we'd spent hours playing outside while wearing our environmental suits. The lawn chairs and barbecue grill, cobbled together from parts Darby had scavenged from old machines. The grill didn't work, of course—there wasn't enough oxygen in the atmosphere to light a fire. But Darby loved to pose for digi-pics next to it, wearing his environmental suit. He was goofy like that.

Meems said the only thing missing was grass. Phinneus explained it was a plant you grew and cut and then grew again and cut. It didn't make much sense.

Off to the side of our yard was the garage, where we stored our two rovers, and next to that was the docking station, where the robot-controlled supply ship from Earth that came every two years would connect to the settlement. I was already looking forward to the chocolate it would bring.

Something caught my eye. A blinking light was moving slowly across the horizon. It was probably a rover from one of the other countries. It was always a little scary to think how close the other settlements were to us. I sometimes wondered what they looked like, as I'd never seen them. We weren't allowed to go past the little cemetery on the edge of our territory; it was far too dangerous.

There was a soft ringing in the distance; it was the meal chime. Salty Bill would be setting breakfast out now.

After that would be morning chores, lessons, lunch, then afternoon chores, free time, supper, then evening chores, and finally bed. The next morning, we would wake up and start the same routine all over again. Sai liked to say a boring day on Mars was a good day.

"We better get moving, Leo," I said. "Um-yums."

It was a baby word I had used for "food." Now I used it on Leo. He knew that word and turned toward me. But before I could take a step, it happened.

A glowing round object hurtled across the sky, a white-hot tail of light streaking behind it. It crashed far away, waves of bright light exploding around it like a halo.

Leo darted under the couch right before the room began to shake.

All around me, the room rocked wildly. I tumbled to the ground. Across the room, the desk holding the communications digi-slate rattled, and the chair in front of it tipped over with a loud crash. Papers on the desk spilled across the floor, and a locker banged open. I decided to stay where I was: it seemed like the safest thing to do.

Then, as suddenly as it had started, it was over.

Everything was still.

I crawled to the window and looked out. A plume of red dust was rising, as if it had been kicked up by whatever had crashed into it. The question was, *what* had crashed? It had looked like a ship, but not like any ship I had ever seen. It was too round, too glowing, too otherworldly.

Too alien.

Feet pounded up the stairs. Sai burst into the room, worry etched into the lines of his face. He must have been in the middle of shaving: he had green shaving cream on one cheek.

"Are you hurt?" he demanded.

I shook my head and then remembered. "Leo!" I cried, looking around.

Scrambling down onto my hands and knees, I peered under the couch. Leo was curled into a tight loaf and stared back at me. I tugged him out, checking him over. He seemed fine.

Then people were running into the room—Darby and Eliana, Trey, Flossy, Vera, and Albie. Albie looked half-awake, his ball cap on backward.

"Sitrep!" Sai barked. It was short for "situation report" and was his way of asking what had happened.

"Something crashed!" I said, pointing out the window. "I think it was an alien ship!"

Everyone looked at me as if *I* was an alien. Everyone except Trey. He and I had always been fascinated by aliens and monsters. We had watched every digi-reel in our collection that featured them.

"Alien?" Trey asked, eyes widening.

I nodded.

"Bell," Sai said, shaking his head. "There's no such thing as aliens."

Technically, he was right. We had colonized the moon and begun to settle Mars. In all that time, we hadn't encountered alien life. But I *knew* aliens existed. Why wouldn't there be something else besides us out here? It just made sense. There were hundreds of billions of galaxies. Surely one of them had intelligent life. (Maybe even alien cats?)

Meems ran in, carrying her portable med kit. She was wearing her bathrobe, and her short gray hair was wet and plastered to her head.

"What happened?" she asked urgently.

"Something crashed," Flossy said.

"He thinks it was an alien ship," Trey added.

"It was definitely an alien ship," I said.

Meems pushed her way forward with her med kit, her pale eyes filled with worry.

"Did you hit your head, Bell?" she asked, her hand in my hair, feeling for bumps.

"No!" I said, shaking her off. "I'm fine!"

"But this silly talk of aliens—"

"I saw the ship!"

"Describe exactly what you saw," she said, like I was describing symptoms. She was our doctor after all.

So I did. I described the circle of light, the bright white

tail, the explosion. How everything shook and Leo was terrified.

"I see," she said, and looked up at Sai.

Sai was rubbing his gray beard, which he did when he was trying to puzzle something out. There were still bits of shaving cream on his face, but he didn't seem to notice.

"Sounds like a meteorite," Eliana said. She was wearing her usual cargo shorts and T-shirt. She liked to wear shorts because she was in and out of environmental suits all day and got hot.

"But it glowed!" I said.

"That's what meteors do when they enter the atmosphere," she explained.

"I'm pretty sure one crashed when you said you'd marry me, Peanut Butter," Darby teased, winking at his wife. "Or maybe that was my heart exploding from happiness?"

She rolled her eyes at him. "Really, Jelly?"

"Peanut Butter" and "Jelly" were their silly pet names for each other. They had fallen in love on the moon. Sai said he'd recruited them to Mars as a package deal. Eliana was super smart; she had helped design the lunar settlement. Darby called himself a jack-of-all-trades.

"Let me through," a voice called loudly.

Phinneus was pushing up to the front with his cane. He was old and moved slowly, but he had a way of making himself heard. He walked to the window and stared out at the plume of dust.

"Whatever it was, it landed near the French settlement," Phinneus said, pointing his cane. "We need to contact them to see if they're all right."

"Absolutely not," Sai said in a firm voice, crossing his arms.

"Sai," Meems said, "maybe we should go take a look."

"It's not our territory. It's not our problem. You know the rules."

There were a lot of rules. They said it was because Mars was dangerous. I knew them by heart. We all did—they were impossible to miss. The grown-ups had taped them in front of the toilet in our bathroom.

SETTLEMENT RULES

- **Do not go outside without a buddy.**
- **Use the alarm bell in an emergency.**
- **Keep a glow stick in your pocket.**
- **Rovers are off-limits for children.**
- **Do not go beyond the flag.**
- **No contact with foreign countries, ever.**

Beneath the typed rules, someone—probably Vera—had added:

ALWAYS PUT THE SEAT DOWN ON THE TOILET!

Vera, who never missed a chance to argue, asked, "Why can't we go see what it is?"

"Because it's too dangerous," Sai said.

"Yeah, it's too dangerous," Albie echoed.

"You just say whatever Sai says!" Vera snapped at him.

"What if someone's hurt?" Phinneus asked.

And then everyone was talking at once, the voices getting louder and louder until I couldn't tell who was speaking. A loud whistle pierced the noise.

I turned to see Salty Bill standing in the doorway, wearing his apron and holding a plastic whistle. He had a kerchief tied over his head, and his long gray ponytail dangled beneath.

"What's the ruckus?" he hollered as the room fell silent.

"An alien ship crashed over there!" I said.

"It was a meteorite," Sai said.

Salty Bill just shook his head.

"I don't care if a pterodactyl flew out of a black hole and landed here. I'm serving breakfast in five minutes. It's the only meal you're getting until lunch," he announced.

Salty Bill turned and stomped out of the room.

Everyone looked around for a minute. And then followed him out.

Aliens or no aliens, no one ever missed a meal on Mars.

Chapter Three

WEEDS

"Do you really think it was an alien ship?" Trey asked me.

We were waiting in line for breakfast.

I nodded. "It glowed."

Trey shook his head in amazement. He had thick, curly hair and bushy eyebrows, which Flossy had offered to pluck. But even she couldn't do anything about the pimples on his face.

He had on his Stanford University sweatshirt; it was one of his favorites. People on Earth seemed to love sending us clothing from where they went to school. I was wearing a sweatshirt from a place called Dickinson College. It used to be Trey's. Most of my clothes were hand-me-downs from him. When I outgrew them, they'd probably be turned into a pillow or something.

"How fast was it going?" he asked.

"Pretty fast," I said, and felt a rush of excitement because Trey was talking to me like he used to.

"Hmm," Trey said, and picked up two doughy green buns from the serving platter. A lot of the food we ate was made from algae.

"I think—" I began, but Trey ignored me and walked away, the conversation over. Disappointment pooled in my stomach, ruining my appetite.

"Are you going to stand there all day?" Salty Bill asked from behind the counter.

Salty Bill was the first person Sai had recruited. Sai claimed that the cook was the most important person on a mission. Good food made for good morale.

I stared at the doughy buns.

"What flavor are they?" I asked.

"Cinnamon," Salty Bill said in a cranky voice. Salty Bill's resting state was cranky.

I put a bun and a handful of freeze-dried plantains on my plate. Then I served myself a cup of algae tea sweetened with honey and headed to the oval table. The grown-ups usually sat at one end, and we sat at the other. Flossy, Vera, and Trey were already sitting at our end.

Meems liked to say the mess hall was the heart of the settlement because a lot happened here. On one side of the room, gray sheets hung on lines to dry. The mess hall was always warm because of the cooking, so it was a good place to dry laundry.

There was a whiteboard on the wall, where the grown-ups kept a list of what was broken. Right now, the list was short—a broken motor in the algae farm, a light out in the communications room, and a clogged toilet in the kids' wing (not my fault!). Sai never let the list get longer than ten items.

Next to the whiteboard was a digi-monitor that usually displayed a live feed of the surface. But the surface camera was broken—nobody seemed to know what had happened to it—and the monitor was turned off.

I slid onto a stool and took a bite of the bun. It was warm and chewy, just the way I liked it. Salty Bill might be cranky, but he sure could cook.

Something rubbed against my ankle, and I looked down. It was Leo.

"You're still hungry?" I asked him. I knew Salty Bill had already fed him.

"Meow meow!" he said, which meant *Yes*.

I snuck him a piece of my bun.

Across the table, Vera was wearing her favorite color: black. It was all she wore lately. Flossy said Vera was trying to be goth, which was an old Earth style. Flossy was something of an expert when it came to Earth customs, especially fashion and slang.

"What do you think of my new outfit?" Flossy asked us. "I copied it from a digi-reel. It's 1970s-style. Isn't it groovy?"

The outfit was like an environmental suit, except tighter-fitting and with a zipper up the back.

"It's nice," I told her.

"It's called a jumpsuit," Flossy told me. "It took me forever to do the zipper."

"I don't know why you bother, Flossy. It's not like anyone is ever actually going to see it," Vera said.

"What do you mean?" Flossy asked. "Everyone can see it!"

"I mean anyone who's actually *interesting*," Vera said, rolling her eyes.

Trey was staring across the room, where Sai and Albie were looking at a clipboard and talking.

"Why does he get to be Sai's apprentice?" Trey asked with a scowl.

Recently, Sai had begun taking on an apprentice. He taught them about running the settlement. Last year, it had been Flossy. Sai had picked Albie a few weeks ago, and Trey had been unhappy ever since.

"Do you think it's because he's older than me?" Trey asked.

Flossy shook her head. "I was the first apprentice, and I'm not the oldest."

Trey frowned. "Why did he pick you anyway?"

"Probably because I have excellent taste in fashion," she declared with a grin.

"I think Sai chose Albie because he's so responsible," I said.

Vera snorted. "I guess I don't have to worry about Sai ever picking me as his apprentice."

Vera didn't exactly have the best judgment. After all, she was the one who had thought it would be fun to prank Salty Bill by switching the labels on all his spices. He still hadn't forgiven her.

"It's so unfair," Trey muttered.

I didn't understand why he cared. The grown-ups only talked about schedules and what needed to be fixed. We kids had way more fun.

"Three-word story," I said.

Flossy gave a little clap.

It was our favorite game: you made up a story, and each person used three words. Trey always managed to get "fart" into the story. It was a real skill.

"I'll go first," I said. "Once upon a . . ."

". . . time, an alien . . . ," Flossy continued.

". . . crashed on Mars," Vera said with a bored expression.

It was Trey's turn, but he wasn't paying attention.

"Trey," I said.

But he didn't say anything. Maybe he hadn't heard me?

"Trey," I said again, tapping his shoulder. He turned to me, his lips thin.

"It's your turn," I told him.

"This is a dumb game," Trey said.

I just stared at him. "That's five words."

Across the room, Sai stood up, holding his digi-slate. He was wearing his Command-issued blue uniform, as usual. He was the only one who ever wore his uniform; he said some habits were hard to break.

"Chore assignments," he called to us. "Gather round."

We crowded around him as he rattled off the chores.

"Flossy, kitchen. Vera, laundry. Trey, dust duty. Bell, algae farm. And, Albie, you're shadowing me."

"Laundry? How thrilling," Vera said, rolling her eyes.

I had nothing to complain about. I loved the algae farm.

But I could tell from the way Trey was standing— shoulders hunched, fingers curled—that he was not happy with his assignment.

"Dust duty? Again? That's the second time this month!" he fumed.

"We can trade," I suggested to Trey. "I'll do dust duty!"

"No trading," Sai said firmly.

"Why can't I apprentice like Albie?" Trey demanded.

"Because you're not ready," Sai said.

"I am so!"

"You're not ready until *I* say you're ready," Sai said, his voice firm.

Trey looked like he was going to say something, but he turned and stomped out of the mess hall without a backward glance.

·✺·

A blast of warm air hit me when I walked through the doorway to the algae farm, Leo padding behind me. The sharp scent of algae tickled my nose. This was my favorite place in the settlement: it was green, and everywhere you looked, something was growing. But mostly I loved it because of Phinneus.

When the Mars Settlement Mission was announced, Sai said he received over ten thousand applications. But when it came time to choose the crew, he threw out the résumés and went looking himself. He said he'd needed people who were problem solvers. People who were used to messy work in difficult conditions. Like plumbers and electricians and farmers. Sai said that was who kept a settlement running. Phinneus was one of those people. He'd been a farmer in New California.

I made my way through the maze of the farm to Phinneus's office. All around the room were massive containers of live algae. The algae was grown in batches depending on what it would be used for: food, fuel, medicine, oil, paper, even soap. The algae also created the oxygen we breathed.

Phinneus was sitting at his messy desk, fast asleep. He slept a lot these days, usually after meals.

"Hi, Phinneus," I said.

He blinked his watery blue eyes open, looking confused.

"Bell," he said, putting his glasses on. "I must have dozed off."

He looked at the notebook in front of him and closed it.

Leo leapt onto the desk and started nibbling on a leafy plant. It was catnip. Phinneus grew it for Leo.

"There's that old lion," Phinneus said, observing Leo. "He's getting fat. You need to stop feeding him scraps."

"He's always hungry," I said. "What's a lion?"

"It's a very large cat," he explained.

"How large?"

He rubbed his chin. "Oh, I don't know exactly. About three meters long, I suppose."

"That's huge! Bigger than Albie! So why do you call Leo that?" I asked. "He's not very big."

"It's his attitude. He acts like a lion. He's fearless," he said, shuffling papers on his desk. On the corner of the desk was a jar of cookies. Phinneus claimed he got hungry when he was working, but I suspected he kept them for us kids.

"Can I have a cookie?"

"Didn't you just have breakfast?" he asked.

"I'm still hungry," I told him, which was the truth.

"You're just like your cat," he said.

"Fearless?"

"Always hungry," he said.

"What are we doing today?" I asked him.

"Shampoo, I think," he said.

Phinneus made shampoo from algae. It smelled nice, but it gave your hair a bit of a green tinge.

"Might as well get started," he said, standing up and grasping his cane.

We walked back to the main area, past the hydroponic setup where Phinneus raised lettuces and herbs. He also had a tub of soil from Earth. I liked the texture of Earth soil, the crumbly softness of it.

"What are you growing?" I asked him. Fuzzy green shoots poked out of the soil.

"Summer squash," he said.

"Socksy!" I said.

Phinneus chuckled. "I don't think I'll ever get tired of hearing you saying that."

"Socksy" was my very own slang for "great." When I was little, I hated wearing socks. To encourage me, the grown-ups would give me a piece of candy every time I put on a sock. After a while, I would put on a sock, walk up to them, and announce "Socksy!" just to get candy. In my head, "socksy" meant "great!" because candy was great. It just sort of stuck.

"Tell me," he asked with a probing look. "How are you

feeling after this morning's excitement? That must have been quite a shock."

"Okay, I guess."

"You know, I don't agree with Sai," he told me.

"Me neither! It was definitely an alien ship!"

Phinneus shook his head. "Not about that. It was most likely a meteorite."

"Oh," I said. That was disappointing.

"I meant about the French settlement," he explained. "We should have contacted them to make sure they were okay."

"But we're not allowed. They're the enemy. That's what everyone says," I said.

"Just because everyone says something doesn't mean it's true," he told me somberly.

"What?" I asked.

"On Earth, I had a large garden where I grew vegetables. Sometimes there would be weeds," he said.

"What's a weed?"

"It's a plant that just starts growing. If you don't pull the weeds out, they can take over a garden. They crowd out the vegetables—kill them—until there's nothing but weeds."

Killer plants? Earth sounded creepy.

"The point is: You have to take care of your garden. Make sure there are no weeds. Do you understand?"

I shook my head; I didn't understand.

"Are there killer weeds on Mars?" I asked.

"Oh, Bell," he said, shaking his head. "What am I going to do with you?"

"Let me have a cookie?"

He sighed.

DATE: 3.6.2091
FROM: CDR Dexter
TO: US Terrestrial Command
MESSAGE: Situation Report

An unidentified object struck the surface at approximately 06:00 hours this morning. No harm to the settlement is noted at this time.

I have not inspected the crash site, as the location was determined to be in a foreign settlement. It is unclear if this was a meteorite or, possibly, an alien craft.

Please advise.

Sai Dexter, COMMANDER
Expeditionary & Settlement Team
United States Territory, Mars

Chapter Four

SECRETS AND GIFTS

The tinkling sound of music bounced around our bedroom a few days later. Albie was working on a new song. He loved making music on his digi-board. This song was bright and warm, like the golden light of the fake illuminated window on the wall. The window looked like the sun beaming down on a pink Mars—a pretty illusion, since we had no windows underground.

"What do you think?" he asked me when he finished.

"It's good," I said.

"It's for Meems's birthday." He looked unsure. "Do you think she'll like it?"

"She'll love it," I said. Meems would like anything we gave her. After all, she'd told me the painted rocks I'd given her for the last two years were lovely.

I didn't know what I was going to do for her this year. It was a few months away, so I had some time to come up with something. But it was hard because I didn't have a talent like everyone else.

Flossy could sew, and Albie made music. Trey could make just about anything with the 3D modeler. And Vera, for all her snarkiness, could draw soulful kittens and sweet butterflies. But me? I wasn't good at anything. I'd probably end up painting another rock.

The lights in the room flickered and abruptly changed from day to night. The window was now black, with fake winking stars. The hallway outside our door was the cool blue of night.

"Light timer must be broken again," Albie said.

The timer that controlled the lights in our wing had been on the fritz lately.

I followed Albie into the corridor where our wing's junction box was. He opened the panel and poked around.

"The control button keeps falling off. Can you get some duct tape from Sai?"

"Sure," I said, and walked down the hall.

As I passed the older kids' room, I heard Trey and Vera talking excitedly through the door. I paused to listen, catching random words.

Rover. Chores. Lunch.

I didn't know what it all meant, but I was jealous anyway.

Because I used to be Trey's person.

We were famous—Trey and I. The story went that when he saw me, he immediately claimed me as his "Bell-Bell." Trey would climb into my crib and entertain me with toys and books, even nap with me. We were inseparable.

I was a late talker, which worried everyone until Meems realized Trey was my voice. Whenever I wanted something, he just got it for me. I didn't need to speak, because I had Trey. Eventually, Meems had to tell Trey to stop doing that.

When I got to Sai's workshop, he was bent over the 3D modeler. I loved the smell in here: hot plastic and sharp metal and oil.

"What are you doing?" I asked him.

He leaned back and rubbed his neck.

"Well, I'm *trying* to make a new part for the primary motor in the algae farm. But I'm not having much success."

I looked around the room: The walls were lined with floor-to-ceiling plastic shelving crammed with all sorts of things. Jars of screws and nails. Boxes of tools. Old engine parts and electrical cords. Glow sticks and glue and all kinds of springy bits. Everything was neat as a pin and organized. Back on Earth, Sai had been in charge of logistics for McMurdo Station, in Antarctica. He knew the importance of every piece of material in our settlement.

"What can I do for you?" Sai asked me.

"I need duct tape. The light timer in our wing is broken again," I said.

Sai sighed and pointed to a shelf. "Over there."

I picked up a roll.

"And be sure to bring the rest of it back," he added. Duct tape was the most prized supply item in the settlement.

"Do you have any ideas about what I can make Meems for her birthday?" I asked him.

"Her birthday? I'm not sure. What did you give her last year?"

"I painted a rock," I said.

"Do that again," he told me, and turned back to his work.

I should have known better than to ask Sai. Meems said he wasn't good at human-ing.

I was on my way to lessons. The grown-ups took turns teaching us in a storage room that had been outfitted with a table and stools. Some of the lessons were digi-slate learning—mathematics and programming and writing—and some were practical. Meems taught us about medicine and first aid. Phinneus instructed us in botany. Darby taught us how to unclog a toilet (he said it was the most important life skill anyone could have).

As I walked past the open door of Meems's room, I heard her call, "Bell, can you come help me, please?"

"Sure," I said. "What do you need?"

"I can't open this," she said, handing me a plastic medicine bottle. Meems had arthritis, and it was always worse in the mornings. "I've told Command not to send us any more childproof bottles, but they don't listen."

I clicked it open, then handed it to her.

"Thank you, Kitten," she said, shaking out some pills. She called me that because when I was a toddler, I used to follow the cats around. One time, she found me curled up with them under a bed, fast asleep.

Mementos from Earth were scattered around her room. A feather from a real bird. Something called a pine cone, which she said came from a tree. Glass marbles. And then there were the framed digi-pics. She had dozens of them arranged on a table. Most were of her in a place with snow. Meems had worked in a remote part of Alaska, and when Sai recruited her to come to Mars, she'd said yes right away. She was already used to cold and isolation.

In one of the digi-pics, Meems was younger and was wearing a flight suit, her hair long and tied back in a ponytail.

"Why did you cut your hair, Meems?"

She laughed, touching her wispy short hair. "Because you don't have time to worry about your hairdo when you're trying to survive on a new planet. Also, we had a terrible lice infestation."

"What's lice?"

"Lice are little bugs that live in your hair and make you itch," she said, and put her hand to her head as if remembering. "They were our stowaways on the ship."

Another digi-pic caught my eye. It was of Meems when she was little. She was sitting on an Earth animal next to an older man with a funny mustache.

"What's this digi-pic about?" I asked her.

"My seventh-birthday party. That's my father."

"But why was there an animal at the party?"

"It was sort of a tradition for children to ride a pony at their birthday party. Like balloons and cake."

"So you had a pony and balloons and cake?"

She smiled. "Carrot cake. My favorite. My mother made it for me every year."

And that's when I knew what I could give Meems for her birthday. I might not have been able to make a song or a drawing, but I could give her something even better.

A sweet memory.

I asked Phinneus if he would help me grow some carrots.

"Why carrots?" he asked.

"I want to make Meems a carrot cake for her birthday.

It's her favorite kind of cake. Her mother used to make it for her."

Phinneus's eyes softened. "You have such a big heart, dear boy. It takes about two months to grow carrots hydroponically, so we should put them in today. Come by after lessons, and we'll do it together."

"Thanks," I told him. "And don't tell Meems about the cake. I want it to be a surprise."

"I won't," he promised.

After lunch, I sat in my room and searched for carrot cake recipes on my digi-slate.

Vera pushed her head in the door. "Psst, Bell!" she said. "Come over to our room!"

"Why?"

"It's a secret."

A secret? Nobody could keep a secret on Mars.

"I'm kind of busy," I told her.

"Come on," she said, and grabbed my arm, tugging me across the hall. I was pretty sure she was the bossiest person on Mars.

As I was pulled into the room, I looked around. I hadn't been in it since Trey had moved. It was easier to just avoid it.

Most of the room looked the same as mine. A plastic rack held Flossy's handmade Earth outfits, and posters of Earth musicians were on the wall by Vera's bed. In the middle of the room was the lumpy fabric chair, another of

Flossy's creations. She called it a beanbag, but there were no beans inside it, just chunks of soft rubber.

Trey's area was easy to spot: his bed wasn't made (he never made it), and his dirty socks were piled on the floor. He hadn't decorated; there wasn't anything on the wall over his bed. It looked so . . . temporary.

"Hey, Bell," Trey said, glancing up from the game he was playing on his digi-slate. He looked almost happy to see me.

"What's up?" I asked.

"So. We need your help," Vera said.

"*My* help?"

"We want to go see the spaceship," she said. "You're the only one who saw it fall. You can show us where it is! Doesn't that sound fun?"

Fun? Were they kidding me?

"It's dangerous to go near the other settlements!" I said.

One of our crew members, a woman named Lissa, had died near the French settlement. I was a little unclear on what had happened because none of the grown-ups liked to talk about it. She was buried in the cemetery with the cats.

"Yes, yes, it's so dangerous, blah-blah-blah," Vera said, rolling her eyes. "Look, how bad can it be? The grown-ups used to work with the other countries. How do you think the rail tunnel got built? It was an international thing."

I shook my head, my stomach churning. "No way. We'll get in so much trouble."

"Remember all the times we talked about alien ships?" Trey asked me.

I nodded. Of course I remembered.

"Now's our chance to actually see one in real life!" Trey said, his voice urgent. "We'll take the rover and go after lunch tomorrow. Be back by supper. No one will even know we've gone."

"But—" I said.

"It'll be fun," Trey promised. "An adventure."

And for a moment, he seemed like the old Trey: the one I shared a room with, the one who knew everything about me. My best friend.

"Come on," he said.

Aw, dust it. I never stood a chance.

"Okay," I said.

Flossy burst through the door, a smile on her face.

"So are you coming with us to see the alien ship tomorrow?" she asked me. "I still haven't decided what I'm going to wear."

"Flossy!" Vera said.

Like I said, it was impossible to keep a secret on Mars.

DATE: 3.11.2091
FROM: CDR Dexter
TO: US Terrestrial Command
MESSAGE: Situation Report

More than one-third of our storage batteries have failed and cannot hold a charge. This could have significant consequences in the event of a power emergency.

Please advise.

Sai Dexter, COMMANDER
Expeditionary & Settlement Team
United States Territory, Mars

Chapter Five

THE RULES

My hands shook as I tugged on my bulky environmental suit. I could barely pull up the zipper; I was too anxious.

Because I couldn't believe we were actually doing this.

Sure, we'd done some dumb things in the past (well, mostly Vera had), but never anything this bad. This was going against every single rule we'd ever learned.

No one else seemed scared, though. Flossy and Vera and Trey looked excited as they stepped into their suits. When they rushed through the air lock to the garage, I hung back.

Did I really want to do this? Aside from getting in trouble with the grown-ups, this was dangerous. Those digi-reels with aliens always ended badly—usually with someone getting eaten. What if the alien had tentacles? I didn't want to be around one of those guys.

Trey stuck his head through the door.

"Aren't you coming?" he asked.

I swallowed hard.

"Uh, yeah. Just getting zipped up," I said, and followed him to the garage, where Flossy and Vera were arguing next to the *Enterprise*.

The *Enterprise* was the smaller of our two rovers. The bigger rover was called the *Yellow Submarine* and was actually painted yellow. Sometimes I didn't get the odd names the grown-ups gave things.

"I have more hours in the rover than you do," Flossy said.

"Well, it was my idea in the first place," Vera insisted, and pushed past Flossy to get into the driver's seat. "So I'm driving."

I should have known it was Vera's idea.

Trey and I got into the back seats and strapped on our four-point safety harnesses.

Then the garage door slid open, and we were moving.

Everyone was quiet as we drove through the settlement, passing the small, sad graveyard where Lissa and the cats were buried. It was like we were all holding our breath, just waiting to get caught. But nothing happened. No one stopped us.

When we passed the flag that marked the edge of our territory, Vera hooted.

"Here we go!" she shouted as she steered over the bumpy Mars terrain.

But all I could think of was how many rules we were breaking. Correction: how many rules we had *already* broken. So far, they were:

Rovers are off-limits for children.

Do not go beyond the flag.

"Are we going the right way, Bell?" Flossy asked me.

I tried to remember the way the ship had raced across the sky to the west. This seemed right. "Yes."

It wasn't too long before we saw a blue-and-white flag.

"There's Finland," Trey said.

It was the closest settlement to ours, and I had never seen the inside of it.

"I'm pretty sure we're going to pass right by the French settlement," Vera said.

"I watched a French digi-reel. All the girls look so stylish. They wear these scarves around their necks," Flossy said.

Trey looked at me, and even through his helmet, I could see him rolling his eyes.

I stared at the landscape. I never got tired of looking at it. There were gently sloping sand dunes and deep canyons. Mountains, craters, and towering hills with jagged outcrops.

Right now, we were driving across a plain studded

with rocks. The sky was yellowish brown, a color Eliana called butterscotch, after an Earth candy.

As the rover bounced along, my stomach churned. I had a bad taste in my mouth and felt queasy.

Aw, dust it.

I was rover-sick.

"Are we almost there?" I asked.

"That's what the kids always say in the Earth digi-reels, Bell!" Flossy said, amused.

Did Earth kids barf in car vehicles? Because I felt like I was going to do just that any minute now.

"I feel sick," I said.

"Sick how?" Flossy asked.

"Rover-sick," I admitted.

"Oh, that's just great," Vera said, and sighed.

Finally, after what seemed like forever, Flossy pointed excitedly.

"I see it!" she said. "That's the French flag."

Up ahead, there was a round pod of a habitat. A red-white-and-blue flag fluttered from a pole.

"Let's get closer," Vera said.

I looked at Trey and shook my head, mouthing, "No." I could tell he didn't think this was a good idea, either.

"Uh, we're not allowed to visit other countries," Trey said.

"We aren't allowed to take the rover, either, but here we are," Vera replied.

Vera pulled the rover alongside the habitat, so that we could look in the hexagon-shaped windows. But there were no lights on.

"Where is everyone?" Vera asked.

"Probably underground," Trey said.

"That's too bad. I really wanted to see a French person," Vera said.

We had never seen anyone from the foreign territories in real life.

"Well, I really wanted to see the scarves," Flossy said, disappointed.

I took a deep breath, staring out my window. Now that we weren't moving, I was starting to feel a little better.

That is, until I saw the person in the environmental suit walking toward us. They were carrying something long and metal with a curved end, which looked like a weapon.

"Uh," I said. My mouth couldn't seem to work right.

"Do you think they look like us?" Trey asked.

"Of course they do," Vera said.

"How do you know?" Trey asked.

"I've seen digi-pics."

"Except they wear cute scarves," Flossy added.

Another person in an enviro suit joined the first one and had a long metal thing, too. That person turned and shook their metal thing at our rover.

"They look just like that!" I shouted, pointing out my window.

Trey gasped. The people shuffle-hopped toward us, gesturing angrily and waving their weapons.

"They don't seem very friendly," Trey said.

"I think we should go," Flossy said. "Now!"

"Right," Vera said, fumbling with the controls.

"It's in park!" Flossy said. "Put it in drive!"

"I'm trying!" Vera cried.

"Hurry," I urged. "They're coming!"

It wasn't fast enough, because they had already reached the rover and were banging on my window. I looked into the face glaring at me from behind the helmet. It was a man, and he looked angry. Fear rushed through me.

"Move! Let me do it!" Flossy yelled, leaning over and knocking Vera's hand away. She shifted the gear into reverse.

Suddenly, we were driving backward, the French people chasing us. Then Vera turned sharply, and we were driving forward, away from the French settlement.

I looked anxiously behind us until the figures were just specks on the horizon.

And then, finally, nothing at all.

The inside of the rover was quiet as it bumped along. No one was talking or laughing. All the excitement had escaped, like air draining from a balloon. I couldn't stop shaking. All I could think was that we had broken another rule:

No contact with foreign countries, ever.

Was having them chase us technically considered contact? It wasn't like we'd talked with them or been invited over for supper.

"What was that thing they were waving at us?" Flossy asked.

"Some kind of weapon," Vera said.

"Maybe a sword? Like from Earth ancient times?" Trey suggested.

I looked out the window and down at the steep sand dune cliff we were driving on top of. I took a deep breath. But it didn't help, because I couldn't shake the fear anymore. It clung to me like a second skin.

"I want to go home," I blurted out.

"You do?" Trey asked.

"Yes," I said, and he must have seen the fear in my eyes.

"Okay," he said, nodding slowly.

"No way!" Vera said. "We came all this way. Besides, we're close to the crash site."

"I think we should take a vote," Flossy said. "I vote we go home."

"Me too," Trey said.

"Me three," I said.

Vera turned to look back at us. There was a furious expression on her face. "This isn't fair!"

"We took a vote, Vera," Flossy said.

"Well, I'm the one driving, and I say—"

But she never finished her sentence. The next thing I knew, we were rolling over and my helmet smacked the window hard and everything turned black. When I opened my eyes, the rover was on its side and everyone was yelling and all I could do was gasp because of the pain in my shoulder. It felt like it was on fire.

"You drove right over the edge, Vera!" Flossy said.

"It wasn't my fault!" Vera shrieked. Her voice seemed even louder in my helmet.

"Are you hurt, Bell?" Trey asked in a panicky voice.

I tried to say something, but when I moved, sharp pain arced through my shoulder, and I screamed.

"Bell's hurt!" Trey shouted.

"Everyone stay calm, just stay calm!" Flossy said. "Shouting won't help anything."

"I am calm!" he snapped at her.

Flossy turned to look at me. "Where does it hurt, Bell?"

"My shoulder," I said with a whimper. "Get me out!"

"The harness hurts?" Trey asked.

"Yes!"

"Hold on!" he said.

Trey undid his harness and scrambled over, looking at mine. He unlatched it, and my body fell toward the ground, hitting the side of the rover. I yelped in pain.

"Are you okay, Bell?" Vera asked.

"What do you think?" I huffed.

"We need to call for help now!" Trey said.

"Well, unless someone happened to steal a digi-comm, we're out of luck," Flossy said. Only the grown-ups had digi-comm devices.

We all looked at Vera. She was the sneakiest one of us.

"I didn't take one!" she said, throwing up her hands.

Of all the times for Vera to be good.

"Aw, dust it," I whispered.

Chapter Six

BAD BORING

"Should we try and walk home?" Vera asked. "We have air canisters."

"We're too far away," Flossy said, studying the GPS. "We don't have enough air to make it back."

"Bell's injured! He'll never make it," Trey said, and I shot him a grateful look.

"Besides, it's safer to stay here," Flossy added. "We still have pressurization and heat."

"For how long?" Vera asked.

"I don't know, Vera," Flossy said.

"But—"

"Vera, just stop!" Flossy hissed in a low voice. "You're scaring Bell."

Which was true.

I tried to get into a comfortable position. Every time I moved, it hurt. Finally, I closed my eyes. I must have fallen asleep because when I woke up, it was dark outside.

"What time is it?" I asked groggily.

"Nineteen hundred hours," Trey said.

We'd missed supper. I wondered what Salty Bill had cooked. I could really go for something warm right now. Like his famous algae biscuits.

"Do you think they've figured out we're gone?" I asked.

"They might not have noticed we missed afternoon chores. But supper? I'm sure everyone knows something's up by now," Flossy said.

She sounded confident, but for some reason it didn't make me feel better. How were they ever going to find us?

"Yeah," Trey agreed. "You know how Sai is. He's probably stomping around looking for us right now."

"I don't know about that," Vera said in a small voice.

Flossy's eyes narrowed. "What did you do?"

"Uh, I may have reset the light timers in the settlement."

Trey's mouth dropped open.

"And all the digi-clocks," Vera added.

"Why?" Flossy asked.

"To give us a few extra hours to explore," Vera said. To be honest, I was kind of impressed. Only Vera could think of something devious like that.

"So you mean they don't even know we're missing yet?" Trey asked.

"Probably not," Vera said. "I reset everything by two hours."

We sat there looking at one another.

"Oh no," Vera said.

"What?" I asked.

She grimaced. "I have to go to the bathroom."

·Ö·

Now I knew what the grown-ups meant about being stuck on the spaceship. It had only been a few hours, and this was pure torture. The first thing I planned to do when I got home was never leave again.

Not to mention, it was boring. And not good boring. It was bad boring.

Good boring was predictable—like doing chores at the same time every day. It was no fun, but you knew what was expected. Bad boring was being bored and having absolutely no idea what was going to happen. Not knowing was scary—scarier than aliens or even French people.

"It stinks in here, and I'm hungry!" Vera said.

Well, at least one thing *was* predictable. You could always count on Vera to complain.

"I can't do anything about that," Flossy said.

"Well, I can," she said.

Vera lifted up a silver backpack. I recognized it. There were emergency packs in every rover, stocked with the basics—medical supplies, water, meal bars, glow sticks.

"Hey!" Flossy said. "Don't eat those yet!"

"Why not?" Vera asked.

"Because we don't know when we're going to be rescued. We should save it for an emergency!"

"This is an emergency!" Vera snapped.

"How hungry can you be anyway? You had lunch!" Trey complained.

"You're not the boss of me," she said.

Vera opened the backpack and shuffled through it. She picked up a meal bar.

"Vera," Flossy said in a low voice.

Vera stared at the meal bar for a long moment and sighed.

"Fine," she said.

Then she put it back and zipped the bag shut.

⚙

I tried to sleep, but I couldn't get comfortable. Every time I moved, pain streaked through my shoulder. And my head was pounding.

"My head hurts," I whispered.

Trey's eyes snapped to me. "Where?"

"Everywhere," I said.

"I think he's dehydrated," Flossy said. "You should drink some water, Bell."

"But I thought we were saving it for an emergency?" Vera asked.

"Like Flossy said, you should drink some water," Trey said in a firm voice.

Flossy pulled out a pouch of water, broke a straw into it, and handed it to me. I looked at it, wondering how much water we had left. How long could we last with that small backpack of provisions—a few energy bars and pouches of water? What would happen when they ran out?

"Are we going to die here?" I asked.

"Of course not!" Flossy said.

"But we'll run out of food in no time! What will we eat?"

"We could always eat you," Trey said.

I frowned at him.

"Well," Vera said, "I did it."

"Did what?" Trey asked.

"I peed in my suit," Vera announced.

"You did what?" Flossy asked.

"It just happened," Vera said, and snorted.

Flossy burst into peals of laughter. I would've laughed, too, except it hurt too much.

But Trey wasn't laughing.

"This isn't funny," he bit out.

"I know," Vera said. "I'm the one in the suit."

But I could tell he was getting angry from the tone of his voice.

"We wouldn't be stuck here if it wasn't for you!" Trey groused. "You should've let Flossy drive! She wouldn't have driven us into a sand dune!"

As their voices filled the rover, I closed my eyes. The grown-ups had been right all along. Mars was dangerous. If we got out of this alive, I would never, *ever* break a rule again.

Then something banged hard against the rover, and Flossy screamed.

Chapter Seven
LEFT BEHIND

Sai's stern face stared at us from the inside of his helmet. Past the dune, I could see the lights of the *Yellow Submarine*. Eliana was at the wheel.

"They found us!" I cried.

"Sai!" Trey shouted.

"See! I told you!" Flossy said.

"If I'd known, I would have held it in," Vera muttered.

After quickly assessing my injury, Sai helped me into the *Yellow Submarine*. Everyone else piled in after me.

The rover was quiet as we headed for home.

"I don't know what you children were thinking," Sai said in a horribly calm voice. It was somehow worse that he wasn't shouting at us.

"We didn't mean to—" Trey began.

Sai cut him off. "You didn't mean to steal the rover?"

Trey flinched.

"How did you find us?" Vera asked.

"There's a tracking device on all the rovers," Eliana explained.

"We put them on after Lissa died in a rover accident," Sai added.

"She did?" Flossy asked, shocked. "I didn't know that."

It was news to me, too.

In fact, the only thing I knew about Lissa was that she had been a nanny. But dying in a rover accident? That was one secret the grown-ups had actually managed to keep on Mars.

"Well, now you know," Sai said. "If we hadn't found you, you could have died in one, too."

No one said anything after that.

"You've fractured your clavicle," Meems told me, studying the handheld X-ray device. "That's your collarbone."

I was lying on the examination table in the small medical bay. The room had all sorts of diagnostic equipment and cabinets with medical supplies. It smelled of antiseptic cleanser and was my least favorite part of the settlement. Nothing good ever happened here. This was where you got shots and had cavities filled.

"And I'm concerned you may have a concussion, too," she said.

"What's that mean?"

"It means your brains got rattled around. I will be waking you up every few hours tonight to make sure you're okay," she said. "It's going to be a long night for both of us."

"Sorry," I said.

"All right, I need to put a sling on your arm to keep it immobilized. It's going to hurt a little."

A little? By the time she was finished, I was panting from the pain.

"How is your pain level from one to ten?" she asked me. "With ten being the worst."

"One hundred!"

She opened a cabinet and surveyed a shelf. "Hmm. I probably should've ordered more painkillers for the supply ship."

The door opened and Phinneus walked in, fear crossing his face when he saw me.

"How bad?" he demanded.

"A fractured collarbone. Maybe a concussion," Meems said.

Phinneus put his hands on my cheeks. He looked like he'd been crying; his eyes were red and puffy.

"I swear, you took five years off my life," he scolded.

"Sorry," I whispered. I seemed to be saying that a lot.

"What were you doing?"

"We just wanted to see the alien ship."

"There is no alien ship," he said. He added softly, "And

you could've died." I'd never heard him sound more disappointed in me.

"Sai said Lissa died in a rover accident. What happened?"

Meems and Phinneus exchanged a long look. It was like they were having an entire conversation without saying a word. Finally, Phinneus sat down with a groan.

"You're having pain again?" Meems asked him.

He nodded.

"Do you want something for it?"

Phinneus waved her off. "It's nothing I can't handle."

"You're so stubborn," Meems said, shaking her head.

"Not as stubborn as some," he said, turning to me. "All right. Where to begin?"

Phinneus smoothed his hands over the top of his cane.

"You know that during the early years of the settlement, we collaborated with the other countries?" he asked me.

I nodded. Everyone knew that.

"It was very collegial. The railway was a joint project between all the countries. It was an incredible achievement. For engineering. But even more so for cooperation. We joked that such a project would never have happened on Earth because of all the red tape."

"What's red tape?" I asked.

"Regulations and rules and all sorts of nonsense that get in the way of progress," he said.

"We have rules here on Mars, though," I said.

"Yes, and I've noticed you're not very good at following them," he pointed out.

Whoops. He was right about that.

"After several years, relations between various countries on Earth started to deteriorate. Countries began fighting over mineral deposits discovered in Antarctica. But here on Mars, things were fine. We were in our own little bubble. Then Lissa died."

"What happened?" I asked.

"Lissa had gone out in a rover with two other people— one French, one Russian. There was an accident, and she didn't make it back," he said, his eyes sad.

"Why?" I asked.

A voice behind me said, "Because they left her behind."

I looked up, startled to see Sai in the doorway.

His face was shuttered, cold. "Lissa was injured, and they left her there to die."

Phinneus sighed and looked down, squeezing his cane.

"Now you know why we have no contact with the other settlements," Sai said.

Meems helped me into my bed. I couldn't lie down because of the sling, so she propped me up with pillows. But I was asleep before she even turned out the light.

I dreamt that I was back in the overturned rover. But it was different this time. Scarier somehow. I looked at the seat next to mine.

Trey was gone. But where?

I looked ahead at the driver's seat. It was empty, too. So was the one next to it.

"Trey? Flossy? Vera? Where are you?"

No one answered.

Then I heard the rumble of a rover. I plastered my face to the window and saw the *Yellow Submarine* driving away.

Without me.

"Wait!" I shouted, banging on the window. "Don't leave me!"

But the rover kept driving, leaving me behind. Just like Lissa.

Alone.

I woke up with a shout, my heart pounding.

Albie's light clicked on, and he was out of bed and by my side.

"Bell," he asked anxiously, "are you in pain? Are you okay?"

"No!"

"You're not in pain?" he asked, confused.

"I'm not okay!" Then the terror and stress of the day caught up to me, and I burst into tears.

"It's okay," Albie said, handing me a tissue. "You're safe now. You're back."

"It was so scary," I whispered.

"Yeah," he said. "I can't imagine. Do you want me to get Meems?"

"No," I said. "She'll be here in another hour to wake me up to check my head."

Albie got back in bed and reached to turn off the light.

"Can you leave it on?" I asked.

"Sure," he said.

I looked around the room. Seeing all the familiar things—Albie's cap, the drawings on the wall, Leo at my feet—calmed me until I could finally breathe again.

"Phinneus told me what happened to Lissa," I said, and explained what I'd learned.

"It makes sense now," he said.

"What makes sense?"

"The grown-ups were all so angry when Lissa died. I didn't understand why," he said, shaking his head. "How could they just leave her?"

"I don't know," I said.

Albie gave a low whistle. "No wonder we aren't allowed to have contact with the other countries."

I stared at the ceiling, remembering the terror.

It wasn't until Albie's snores filled the air that I felt safe enough to fall asleep again.

[VIA SECURE COMMUNICATION]

DATE: 3.15.2091
FROM: CDR Dexter
TO: US Terrestrial Command
MESSAGE: Situation Report

Due to an accident, Rover 2.0 *Enterprise* is
permanently disabled. We only have one working
rover now.

    Please advise.

           Sai Dexter, COMMANDER
           Expeditionary & Settlement Team
           United States Territory, Mars

Chapter Eight

ANIMALS

For the first few days, I spent most of my time sitting in bed propped up with pillows, my arm in the sling.

I worked my way through the library of digi-reels, avoiding the alien ones. And I had my share of visitors.

Flossy usually brought me breakfast and a cheery smile. Vera brought me lunch and gossip. Meems checked on me every few hours. Phinneus read to me. Eliana and Darby popped by and played cards with me (Eliana always won). Salty Bill delivered supper, and even Sai stopped by to see how I was doing. Leo was my constant companion, happy to lie with me on the bed. Especially when I shared my food with him. But there was someone who didn't visit: Trey.

It stung.

I think Albie tried to make up for it. He was always there to help. Whether it was to fluff my pillows or cut up my food (since I was now one-handed) or help me put on my clothes. No wonder Sai wanted him to be his apprentice. He never once complained.

I was half dozing in bed when Phinneus walked in carrying a book.

"How are you feeling?" he asked, studying me with sharp eyes.

"My shoulder really hurts," I said.

"I'm not surprised," he said. Then he handed me a book. "I thought you might like this."

It was called *Animals of the World* and was full of pictures of Earth creatures. As I flipped through it, Phinneus petted Leo.

"You're a fine boy," he said, and I looked up.

"Thanks," I said.

"I was talking to Leo," he teased.

That's when I noticed the thick white bandage on his arm.

"What happened to your arm?" I asked.

"Alligator skin," he said.

The lack of humidity on Mars made skin dry and itchy. Meems had dubbed it "alligator skin." The grown-ups seemed to suffer from it more than we kids did.

"It's to be expected," he said. "We're all getting old."

"What does that mean?"

"Old skin is thin."

I'd never really thought of Phinneus as old. He'd

always looked the same to me: white hair, glasses, warm smile, cane.

"Would you like to see my favorite animal?" he asked me, nodding at the book.

"Sure," I said.

He paged through it, then held it out for me to see. There was a picture of a small, furry animal with floppy ears. The writing beneath it said *The Rabbit.*

"There were lots of those where I lived in New California," Phinneus said with a smile. "They always came hopping out at dusk. We used to call it the Bunny Hour."

"Do you wish you could go back?" I asked him. Not that it was an option; none of us could ever return to Earth. Our bodies were permanently altered from living here. Meems joked that it was a one-way ticket to Mars.

"I did in the beginning. But very rarely these days," he said, looking thoughtful. "Mostly I miss Chinese food."

"Chinese food?"

"It's delicious," he said. "There's nothing tastier than beef chow fun."

"Do you miss your old home?" I asked him.

"Not really," he said. "It didn't feel like home after Rose died."

"I don't ever want to leave," I told him, remembering the French people in the environmental suits chasing us. "It's too scary!"

"Oh, Bell." Phinneus sighed, leaning heavily on his cane. "There is more to life than this settlement."

I shook my head.

"After all, if I hadn't left Earth, I never would have met you," he said with a smile. "And you, my dear boy, were worth the trip."

He patted the pockets of his sweater. "I nearly forgot. I brought you something else."

"You did?"

"Cookies!" he said, pulling out two cookies wrapped in algae paper napkins. He handed me one.

I nibbled on it.

"Are cookies as good on Earth as they are on Mars?" I asked him.

"They're better on Mars," he confided.

"Really?"

He winked. "If I said anything else, Salty Bill wouldn't make any more cookies for me!"

We both laughed because he was right.

I spent hours poring over the animal book. I loved learning about Earth animals. They were awesomely strange.

Like giraffes. Why didn't they tip over with those long necks? Or snakes. How did they move, since they didn't have legs? And penguins. Did they really live on floating pieces of ice?

But the lions were my favorite. How could I not love the big cats? They were social and lived in a group called a pride. They helped each other and raised their cubs communally. They sounded just like us. All our grown-ups had raised us together. One sentence stood out to me:

Lions who are rejected by their pride do not survive long.

The more I learned about Earth animals, the more everyone started to resemble them in my eyes. Sai was a lion, of course. Darby and Eliana were wolves (which mate for life). Meems was a protective mother cat, and I was her kitten. Flossy was a beautiful peacock in her lovely clothes. Of course, Vera was a sneaky fox. Trey was a loyal dog. Salty Bill was easy: he was a cranky ostrich. But Phinneus? I couldn't quite decide what he was. Or Albie for that matter.

I was still thinking about it a few days later when Albie and I were getting ready for bed. He turned off the light. After a few minutes, he started to snore lightly, and I clicked my light on.

"Albie!"

"What? Was I snoring again?" he asked.

"Yes, but that's not why I woke you up! I figured it out!" I told Albie. "Phinneus is a bee!"

"What's a bee?"

"It's an Earth insect with wings. Bees make honey to eat, and Phinneus grows algae for us to eat. See, Phinneus is a bee!"

"If you say so."

"Although he's definitely got some whale in him, too. Whales are very smart."

"Good to know," Albie said, and yawned. "Now turn off the light. I need to get some sleep. I've got to fix that air scrubber first thing tomorrow. It's broken again."

The air scrubbers removed the carbon dioxide we created by breathing. Too much was dangerous.

"Okay," I said, and clicked my light off.

I lay there in the dark. A few minutes later, Albie's snores filled the room.

"Albie!" I shouted.

Albie blinked. "What's wrong?"

"I got it! You're an elephant! A noisy elephant!"

He threw his ball cap at me.

·ö·

Finally, at the end of the week, there was a knock at my door.

"Come in," I called, expecting it to be Flossy or Vera.

I looked up to see Trey in the doorway. He had on a sweatshirt from Fordham University.

"Hi," I said, surprised.

"Uh, yeah, it's laundry day. I'm here to get the sheets."

It was really nice of him.

"Thanks," I said.

Trey looked around the room. "You kept the map up," he observed.

"Of course," I said.

The map hung over my bed. Trey and I had created it together. It had started as a way to get us out of Meems's hair. We were young and bouncing off the walls, so she gave us a gigantic piece of paper and told us to draw a map of our ideal settlement on Mars. Most of our inspiration came from Earth digi-reels. There was a castle with a moat and drawbridge, skyscrapers, a racing track for rovers, a monorail, and dozens of other things we thought a perfect Mars needed. We'd added sections over the years, so that now it sprawled over a huge area of the wall.

"We never did add that tree house," Trey said almost wistfully.

"We could still do it," I said. "I have some paper!"

He shook his head. "You need to move. I have to get the sheets off the bed."

After I got into a chair, I watched as he stripped the sheets.

"So how have you been?" I asked him.

"What do you mean?"

"I haven't seen you since the accident. What's new?"

"Nothing," he said, tugging off the bottom sheet and tossing it to the floor.

I tried again. "What have you been doing?"

"Chores," he said, pulling a pillowcase off.

"Just chores?"

"That's all I have time for. We got punished with extra ones for taking the rover," he said bitterly.

"Oh," I said in a small voice.

"Except you, of course. You get to lounge around all day."

"I'm hurt!" I protested.

"I told Vera we shouldn't have taken you in the first place," Trey said with a sneer. "Now I'll never get to be Sai's apprentice."

"What are you talking about?"

Trey whirled on me furiously. "Sai blames us for you getting hurt. He said we're older and we should have known better."

"But—"

Trey grabbed the dirty sheets in an angry armload and stomped out of the room.

"—it wasn't even my idea," I whispered to no one.

As his footsteps faded, I knew I'd been right about Trey being a dog.

Because he had a terrible bite.

Chapter Nine

EMERGENCY

Sai gave us the same boring speech about safety once a year. No one really paid much attention to it. But after the alien/meteorite crash and the rover incident, Sai was now on a personal mission to make sure everyone was up-to-date on emergency protocols.

We had to carry a glow stick in our pocket (Sai would stop and check us). We had to make sure our enviro suits were clean and hung up and loaded with a fresh oxygen canister, and that our shoes were always close to our beds, and on and on and on. It was annoying but tolerable.

Until it wasn't.

I was lying in bed, fast asleep. After a few weeks of rehab with Meems, my sling was finally off, and while I still had occasional twinges of pain, it was nice to be able to sleep lying down again.

That is, until an alarm blared through the corridors,

jerking me wide-awake. Right away, I knew it was the emergency alarm. The whole settlement was rigged with them. An emergency could be anything from an injury to a fire. Whatever it was, everyone was supposed to rush to that location to help.

As the alarm blared through the air, I realized Albie's snores had officially met their match. I squinted at the glowing digi-clock.

"It's oh-three-hundred!" I said, and groaned.

"Let's go," Albie said, slapping his ball cap on and staggering out of bed.

When we made it to the source of the alarm—the mess hall—everyone was standing around in their pajamas, looking half-asleep. Everyone except Sai, who was alert, dressed in his uniform, and staring at his digi-watch.

"What's going on?" I shouted. "What's the emergency?"

"This is a drill," Sai explained.

We hadn't had an emergency drill in years. In fact, I only remembered ever having two.

"We're still missing Flossy and Vera," he said.

I sat at a table next to Phinneus. He was leaning against his cane and wearing his blue button-up sweater over his pajamas. If a piece of clothing could perfectly describe a person, this sweater was it for Phinneus. It was fuzzy, with fraying threads and two missing buttons. But it was soft and comforting and always made me feel safe. When I was little and had nightmares, Phinneus would tuck that sweater around me and read to me until I fell asleep again.

"I believe you children have caused Sai to lose his mind," Phinneus told me in a loud voice.

"Why do we have to do this in the middle of the night?" Eliana complained. She was wearing her pink pajamas.

"Because it's Sai, Peanut Butter," Darby said, and gave her a kiss on the nose.

Finally, Vera and Flossy came running in, and Sai turned off the alarm.

He shook his head at them.

"It took you five minutes longer than everyone else," Sai told them.

"Wait. This isn't an emergency?" Flossy asked in confusion.

"No. But it could have been," Sai said. "We need to tighten up our safety protocols around here."

"I don't believe this," Vera muttered.

But Sai didn't hear her. Or maybe he pretended not to.

"Next time," he said ominously, "move faster."

I looked over at Albie. *Next time?*

Aw, dust it.

Everyone was exhausted the next morning. I heard Salty Bill tell Sai if he did an emergency drill in the middle of the night again, he could cook his own breakfast.

Then it was time for chores. Meems wouldn't let me do anything strenuous. No heavy lifting. No bending for hours in the farm. Which left only one option: dust duty.

The dust on Mars was fine and got into everything. It stung eyes and burned skin and caused dust cough. So there were filters to collect the dust in the air vents. They needed to be emptied every day. It was tedious but necessary.

I grabbed a bucket and started my rounds. It was pretty simple: just open each vent, and empty the dust into a bucket. Today there wasn't much.

Even though working in the farm was my favorite chore, I didn't mind dust duty. It was easy, and I liked getting to go around the whole settlement. I worked my way from room to room, emptying filters one by one. When I walked into the generator room, Darby was standing on a ladder, fiddling with something high on the wall. He was wearing overalls and a tool belt.

"That's the wrong node for that air scrubber, Jelly!" Eliana shouted up to him.

"No, it's not, Peanut Butter," he said.

On Earth, Darby had been a general contractor, which meant he could fix just about anything.

"I'm telling you it's the wrong one," she said with her hands on her hips.

"I replaced them three seasons ago, remember?" he said as he climbed down.

"Did you put it in the Record?" Eliana asked.

Darby gave her a hopeful smile. "Maybe?"

The Record was where changes and improvements to the settlement were recorded. Because while most of the grown-ups could do a little of everything—cooking, gardening, plumbing—each one had a primary responsibility. If that person was unavailable, the Record would help someone else figure out what to do when something broke.

"You're hopeless," Eliana said with a wry smile. "What am I going to do with you?"

"Keep me?" he asked before he swooped in and kissed her.

Ewww. Yeah, time to get moving.

My next stop was the algae farm. Phinneus was puttering around in the hydroponic section.

"How are the carrots coming along?" I asked him. "Do you think they'll be ready in time?"

"Yes," he said. "Which reminds me. I have something for you."

"You do?" I asked as I followed him back to his cluttered office.

"I forgot I even brought it with me," he said, handing me a wooden box.

I opened the lid. Inside were paper cards.

"Is it a game?" I asked.

"It's a recipe box," Phinneus said. "It belonged to my wife."

"What's a recipe box?"

"It's an old Earth way of keeping recipes. Each card is a different dish."

"Oh," I said.

"See?" he said, and picked up a card. "This was her recipe for carrot cake."

I could read the title: *Yummy Carrot Cake.*

But the recipe was hard to make out. It was written in a loopy hand.

"What language is this?" I asked Phinneus.

"It's English."

"It doesn't look like English," I said.

He chuckled. "It's a way of writing called cursive. If you were in school on Earth, you would know how to read cursive."

"Good thing I'm on Mars," I said.

He burst out laughing. "Do you know what? Rose would have loved you."

"Really?" I asked.

"We couldn't have children of our own," he said wistfully. "It was our greatest regret."

"Well, now you have all us kids," I pointed out.

His eyes softened. "Too true. Do you want to know a secret?"

I nodded.

"After Rose, you, dear Bell, are the best thing to happen in my life," he said.

"Well, after Leo, you're the best thing to happen in my life," I told him.

He shook his head and smiled.

·❂·

My last stop was the train tunnel.

The train connected all the settlements. It had been built as a joint project by the five founding countries—the United States, France, Finland, Russia, and China. They'd attempted to build a train track on the surface, but complications caused them to have to move the whole thing underground. Phinneus was right: it was an engineering wonder. Too bad we didn't use it anymore.

When I slid open the door to the train tunnel and stepped inside with my bucket, an icy blast of air hit my face. The tunnel was kept pressurized but not heated, and the air smelled rusty.

I snapped a glow stick and held it up. There in the darkness was our train, Percy. Eliana had named it after an Earth digi-reel about talking trains. Percy was designed to hold cargo because most of the early investors wanted to mine Mars for its riches—opals, gold, iridium, palladium, and other minerals.

Even though we weren't permitted to visit the other

settlements, Eliana still made sure the train was in working order. When we were younger, she would even let us drive it. We never went far—just to the second curve and back. One time, I honked the horn as we went around the curve, and someone farther down the tunnel honked back. Trey and I had always wondered which country the person was from.

My stomach was growling—it was nearly lunchtime—so I stopped reminiscing and got to work emptying the filter. I was about to leave when I saw something out of the corner of my eye. I squinted into the inky blackness of the tunnel and then froze when something stared back at me.

Something with glowing green eyes.

Except people didn't have glowing eyes.

But I bet *aliens* did.

The bucket fell from my hand, spilling dust.

Could the aliens have survived the crash and somehow gotten into the tunnel? Were they even now infiltrating our settlement? Would they eat us or turn us into mushrooms or something even worse? (Although what was worse than being turned into a mushroom?) And what did they look like? Did they have big teeth and sharp claws? Were they slimy? Did they spit poison?

My head was spinning. I was getting ready to make a run for it when I blinked. And the eyes disappeared.

I held up my glow stick, looking around the shadows,

but there was nothing. Had it even been real? Or had I imagined the whole thing?

Before I could investigate, an alarm started blaring. No doubt it was Sai with another of his emergency drills.

I left the tunnel, and as I made my way toward the alarm, I saw Trey and Vera and Flossy walking down the corridor. No one was in a hurry. I fell into step with them.

"I think this is Sai's way of punishing us for the whole rover thing," Flossy said.

"We're going to be doing emergency drills for the rest of our lives," Vera said bitterly.

While there had been no more middle-of-the-night drills, we'd had two alarms this week.

The source of this one was the generator room, but when Flossy went to open the door, it didn't budge.

"Huh," she said. "It's locked."

"What do we do?" I asked.

"Beats me," Vera said.

So we just stood around and waited for someone to tell us what to do.

Meems came rushing down the hall, carrying her med kit.

"It's locked," I explained. "We can't get inside."

Her face scrunched up. "Locked? That doesn't make any sense."

"Well, it is," Vera said, jutting out her chin. "Sai just wants to torture us."

Meems banged on the door. "Hello? Anyone in there?"

No one answered, and the alarm kept blaring.

"Maybe the alarm malfunctioned," Meems said.

Just then, Phinneus came down the corridor. He was moving more slowly than usual, using one hand to steady himself with the cane while the other touched the wall.

"What are you all doing out here when the alarm is coming from the generator room?" he asked.

"The door's locked," Meems told him. "The alarm must have malfunctioned."

He stared at the door and then looked at Meems.

"Check the carbon dioxide level," he said.

Confusion flashed across her face. "Carbon dioxide?"

"Quickly!" he urged.

Meems scrambled for her med kit. She pulled out an instrument, holding it to the crack below the door. A red light started blinking.

"Oh no!" Meems cried, her face pale. "The air scrubber failed!"

Every room had a carbon dioxide sensor. If it detected a dangerous amount of carbon dioxide, it locked the room to protect the rest of the settlement.

"Help me open the door!" Meems ordered quickly. "They've probably passed out from the carbon dioxide!"

We pushed at the door again and again, but it was heavier than it looked. None of us were strong enough.

Then Albie's big body was barreling down the hall. He was wearing his enviro suit and carrying his helmet.

"What's going on?" he yelled. "Sai said he would meet me topside."

"The air scrubber failed and they're locked inside!" Meems shouted. "We can't open the door!"

"Move!" Albie ordered, putting the thin helmet over his head.

He took a few steps back and threw himself at the door. It crashed open. Huh. Maybe he *would* make a good football player.

On the floor were the motionless bodies of Sai, Eliana, and Darby.

"Hurry!" Phinneus shouted. "Get them out and shut the door!"

Albie dragged them out. With quick efficiency, Meems put masks on them and hooked them up to the oxygen.

Eliana was the first one to open her eyes. She seemed confused and tried to pull off the mask. Meems batted her hands away.

"Keep breathing," she encouraged.

A heartbeat later, Darby groaned. "My head is killing me!"

Then Sai took a deep, labored breath but didn't open his eyes. "Sitrep?" he whispered in a hoarse voice.

"The air scrubber failed. You almost died," Meems said, her voice rising. "All of you almost died!"

Darby looked at his wife and grabbed her hand. "Are you okay, Peanut Butter?"

She looked at him tiredly.

"I told you that was the wrong node, Jelly."

DATE: 4.28.2091
FROM: CDR Dexter
TO: US Terrestrial Command
MESSAGE: Situation Report

I am in receipt of your comm regarding the updated time of arrival for the resupply ship. We will be standing by.

Sai Dexter, COMMANDER
Expeditionary & Settlement Team
United States Territory, Mars

Chapter Ten

ALGAE DAYS

I stared at the goopy green sludge. It wasn't very appetizing.

"Algae porridge again?" Vera complained.

Albie just shoved the food into his mouth. "It's not that bad," he said.

"Speak for yourself," Trey said. His teeth were green from the porridge.

We'd been eating the same meals for the last few days: algae porridge for breakfast, algae stew for lunch, and algae loaf for supper. We were all pretty sick of it. (Especially the algae loaf.)

"I can't wait until the ship gets here," Flossy said, staring at her bowl.

The weeks before the supply ship arrived were always hard. By now, we'd run out of all the good provisions—chocolate, sugar, freeze-dried fruits, salt, cinnamon, maple syrup—just about everything that made life worth living. It's not that we would ever starve: we had two storage rooms full of MREs (meals ready to eat) that we could live on for years. But they weren't very tasty. And, of course, we had algae and the vegetables that Phinneus grew.

"I miss chocolate," Vera said.

"Me too," Albie said. "And honey."

"I miss bread made with Earth flour," Flossy said.

"Jam," Trey said. "That strawberry kind."

"What about those little oranges?" I said. "Those are my favorite."

"Mandarin oranges," Flossy said.

Across the room, Sai stood up to make an announcement.

"No regular chores this morning," he said. "It's harvest."

All us kids groaned.

A few times a year, Phinneus grew a big batch of algae. When it was ready to be harvested, everyone had to drop what they were doing and help out. No one liked it. But there was no getting out of the work because we were making something absolutely vital to the survival of the settlement.

Toilet paper.

With eleven people, we went through a *lot* of the stuff. Also, we would make a version of kitty litter for Leo.

Albie tried to rally us.

"Let's go. The sooner we start, the sooner we're finished," he said.

"I hate my life," Vera muttered.

Even Flossy seemed to wilt a little.

Processing the algae into toilet paper was no fun. You had to pour the algae through a machine that stripped out the water. Then you spread the algae paste thinly on plastic sheets to dry. After that, you had to cut it up into small squares. It was a hot, messy, miserable all-day affair, and if it wasn't done correctly, you ended up with scratchy, bumpy toilet paper.

As I stood up to follow, Sai called, "Bell, you'll be helping Salty Bill in the kitchen."

"How come Bell gets out of harvest?" Trey asked, a mutinous expression on his face.

"Because his collarbone still isn't strong enough, thanks to your little outing," Sai replied.

"I can help! I feel fine!" I insisted.

"Absolutely not," Meems said in a firm voice.

Trey didn't even look at me. He just stomped out.

Salty Bill had modeled the kitchen after the one on a submarine he had worked on for years. It was long and narrow, with a walk-in storage closet at one end. Every bit of space was used as efficiently as possible. It was Salty Bill's kingdom, and we were only allowed to use it with his permission. He was very particular. Something put away in the wrong place resulted in a lot of yelling.

In spite of this, it was usually fun to help in the kitchen. I liked the stirring and mixing and measuring, and I loved the scents—the sweet-spiciness of cinnamon, the cake-batter smell of vanilla, the doughy smell of fresh-baked bread.

But today Salty Bill was crankier than usual, and that was saying something. Every time he opened the storage closet door, he slammed it shut again, muttering about having nothing to cook with.

"No flour," he said. "No garlic powder. No baking soda."

While eating was hard on us, making meals was hard on Salty Bill.

"There had better be salt on that supply ship," he grumbled.

Once during the early years, Earth Command had forgotten to pack salt on the supply ship, and Salty Bill had hit the roof. That's how he got his nickname.

"Can we make something different than algae loaf for supper tonight?" I asked him.

Salty Bill stared at the empty shelves. "I guess we can try to make pasta. Get some algae."

I grabbed a few dried-algae blocks. They always smelled a little funny. Meems said they reminded her of swimming in the lake when she was a child. I still couldn't quite picture a lake. I'd never seen that much water in my life.

We broke the blocks into chunks and put them in the blending machine, adding water. Then we rolled out the algae dough, sliced it into long threads, and put it in boiling water.

"What to do for sauce?" Salty Bill asked, wiping his hands on his apron.

"I don't think Phinneus has any tomatoes," I told him.

Salty Bill sighed. "I miss the days when I could take the train to another settlement and get a cup of sugar."

"Really?" I asked.

He pursed his lips. "Well, that didn't happen often. But it was nice knowing we had the option."

Then he did the strangest thing: he laughed.

"One time, I was trying to make bread and didn't have any yeast. So I went to the French settlement and asked to borrow some. You know what they did?"

I shook my head.

"They gave me some and a basket of baguettes!"

"What's a baguette?"

"It's a really long loaf of bread," he said, holding his arms out wide. "Just about the most delicious thing I've ever tasted." He seemed to catch himself. "Well, those days are long gone."

I thought about other things that were gone.

"What was Lissa like?" I asked.

Salty Bill looked at me sharply. "Why do you want to know?"

"Because I don't remember her," I said. "I was too little."

He stroked his beard. "She was always happy. And she loved waffles."

"I love waffles!" I said.

"It was terrible when she died," he said, shaking his head. "Sai took it the hardest."

The timer went off on the cooker.

Salty Bill poured the algae pasta into a strainer, then put some in a bowl for us to try. We both took a bite.

"Well?" he asked. "What do you think?"

I forced myself to swallow. It was terrible.

"That bad?" he asked.

I nodded.

He picked up the bowl of pasta and tipped it into the trash.

"Looks like I'm making algae loaf," he said. "Again."

·ö·

That night after supper, we kids gathered in the recreation room to watch an Earth digi-reel. We had amassed a large collection. Detective stories. Dramas. Romances. Mysteries. Horror. Cooking shows.

Right now, we were watching a courtroom drama. It was a really old one—from the 1980s. It featured people who were called attorneys. Instead of fighting with a sword or a gun, attorneys used words. They won fights by persuading people. I was fascinated by this.

"Look! She's wearing a pantsuit!" Flossy said excitedly, pointing to the attorney on the screen. Flossy was sitting in her usual spot on the couch. Next to her was Albie.

I was sitting on the floor, petting Pup, a small robot who made a happy doglike sound when you petted him. Sai said he was the best dog ever because he could walk himself.

"What's wrong with her shoulders?" Albie asked.

The shoulders of the attorney's jacket were all puffed up.

"They're supposed to look that way! The 1980s were so fashionable!" Flossy said with a swoony look. "I just love the olden days."

"I would never wear anything like that," Vera said from where she was lying on the floor, her head on a cushion.

"What if it was black?" Flossy asked her.

"No way. It would still have those weird pillow shoulders," Vera said.

I agreed with Vera that the pillow shoulders were weird. (And they looked uncomfortable.) But stranger to me was that almost all the people had very pale skin. Here on Mars our skin colors were varied. From darker than me (Darby) to lighter than me (Vera) to just about like me (Sai).

"Oh, look at her hair," Flossy said, pointing at the screen.

There was a lady with long red hair.

"Does she put paint on her hair to turn it red?" I asked.

Flossy shook her head. "That's her actual hair, silly."

I had never seen a person with red hair in real life.

"You mean it grew that way?" I asked.

"Yes," she said. "There are people on Earth who have red hair. I've seen digi-pics."

"You can't believe everything you see, Flossy," Vera scoffed. "It's probably fake. Like the window behind the curtains."

She was referring to the long cream-colored drapes that Meems had hung years ago. When we were little, she'd told us not to pull on them because there was a fragile window behind them. Of course, Vera didn't listen and opened the curtains to reveal . . . nothing. There was no window. Meems had just hung the curtains to make the room feel more Earth-like. The adults hadn't grown up underground like us, and were funny about it sometimes.

The scene transitioned, and the attorney was in a place that I knew was called a restaurant. It was like our mess hall, only bigger and fancy. There was a sheet on the table, with a flower. I knew what a flower was but had never seen one of those in real life, either. On the table was a slice of pie with some kind of golden crust.

"What is that food they're eating?" Albie asked, leaning forward.

"Ooh! Ooh! I know! That's a quiche!" Flossy said.

"That looks delicious," Vera said. "What's it made of?"

Flossy screwed up her eyes as if trying to remember. "Um, cheese and spinach and a lot of eggs."

"What are eggs?" Trey asked, looking up from the game he was playing on his digi-slate. It was his favorite: you had to shoot asteroids before they hit you.

I knew the answer to that one. "They come from a chicken bird," I said.

"I would love to go to a restaurant place," Flossy said, a little wistful.

"I'd like to go anywhere but here!" Vera said.

"Really? Look what happened the *last* time you left the settlement," Albie said pointedly.

Vera frowned at him. "You sound more like Sai every day."

"What's that supposed to mean?" Albie asked.

"You do kind of sound like him," Flossy agreed.

"Yep," Trey said.

Albie looked at me. What could I say?

"It's true," I said.

"The point is," Vera said, "I don't want to spend my entire life here!"

"Why not?" I asked. I didn't understand her.

"I don't want to spend my life making toilet paper! I want to eat something besides algae loaf! I want to meet other people!" Vera said.

"Remember how they chased us at the French settlement?" I asked her.

But Vera was getting worked up. There was no reasoning with her when she was like this.

"Who are we going to fall in love with?" Vera demanded.

"Love?" Albie asked.

"Yes," she said. "Don't you want to fall in love?"

"Uh, I've never really thought about it," Albie admitted, taking off his hat and scratching his head.

"Well, I want to fall in love!" Vera exclaimed.

"Not me," Trey said.

"Me neither," I said.

"I want to fall in love wearing a pantsuit! Or maybe a poodle skirt, like from the 1950s," Flossy said. "What do you think? Pantsuit or poodle skirt?"

We all just looked at her.

Chapter Eleven

SUPPLY FEAST

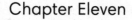

Everyone gathered in the COR to watch the supply ship docking. It was always thrilling to witness the robot-guided ship landing. The way it dropped from the sky and inched slowly forward until it clicked into the air lock.

I stood next to Flossy at the window.

"I hope they sent eye shadow," she said.

"What's that?" I asked her.

Her face scrunched up. "It's like a paint for your eyelids. It makes you look mysterious."

"Three minutes until *Galatea Two* landing," Sai announced.

He was tracking the supply ship's progress on his digi-slate, a strained expression on his face. If the ship miscalculated, it could land dozens of kilometers from the settlement. That would mean days—maybe even weeks—of traveling by rover to fetch the supplies. It had only happened once in all these years, but I guess once was enough.

"It's on track," Sai said. "Nine, eight, seven—"

I watched as the ship descended, throwing up dust everywhere. A loud roar filled the air. Then there was a thud as it docked, and the settlement shook.

Everyone cheered. Sai looked so relieved, he actually smiled.

"All right," he said. "Let's start unloading the old girl."

There was something for everyone.

Powdered chocolate and chili powder and lots of salt for Salty Bill. Cucumber and radish seeds for Phinneus. Some kind of medical gadget that took your temperature for Meems. A new 3D printer for Sai. There was even something for Leo: shrimp-flavored cat dental treats. And, of course, there were packages for the grown-ups from their Earth families. One of Darby's uncles always sent him woolen socks, and Eliana's younger sister sent her pictures drawn by her niece and nephew.

Then there was everything else: tubing and wiring and spare parts galore, bags of flour, glow sticks, soft cotton sheets, warm fleeces, underwear, socks, and shoes in various sizes. A box of eyeglasses because the adults were having a hard time reading these days. Two cases of toothpaste. Pens with real ink. Cotton swabs. Sharp scissors, razor blades for shaving, tubes of coconut-flavored lip balm.

"Have you seen any skin moisturizer?" Meems asked Sai as she checked things off her list.

"I haven't run across it yet," Sai told her.

"Where's our box?" Vera demanded.

There was always a box of stuff just for us kids. When we were younger, the box had contained toys and clothing. But as we'd grown older, different things had appeared. Puzzles and books and digi-reels and barrettes and deodorant. Sometimes they sent odd things: a kite and a bag of Super Balls were in the last shipment.

"I think I saw it in the back," Sai said.

An hour later, we found the box behind the container of Earth soil that Phinneus had ordered. We crowded around it, eager to see what was inside. There was a black knit beanie, dice, a board game, something called pimple cream, a digi-case of pop songs, colored pencils, drawing paper, mirrored sunglasses, plastic bracelets, fingerless gloves, a stack of graphic novels, chewing gum, a digi-player with games, and celebrity magazines.

"Look!" Flossy cried in delight, holding up two thick knit socks that were missing the feet.

"What are they?" I asked.

"Real leg warmers!"

Although we would share most everything, we were each allowed to have one item as ours. Flossy claimed the leg warmers, and Vera took the black knit beanie. Trey got the digi-player of games, and to no one's surprise, Albie wanted the pop songs.

At the bottom of the box was a blanket. It wasn't like any blanket I'd seen before. It was made of small squares of fabric, all pieced together. The fabric was soft and in different shades of blue and green. There was a note pinned to it:

To the children of Mars,
    We hope you like it! We made it ourselves.
        Your friends,
        Mrs. Taylor's sixth-grade class
        Lincoln Elementary School
        New California, USA

"That's a quilt," Meems told me.

I looked at it.

"It's a special kind of blanket," she said. "It takes a lot of work to make one. Usually a group of people get together to sew it. My grandmother used to make them with her friends."

That seemed sweet.

"I'll take this," I said, and picked up the quilt.

⚙

Phinneus told me that on Earth there was a celebration called Thanksgiving, when people ate turkeys and played football. I thought it would be sad to eat turkeys; they looked cute. Here on Mars, we had Supply Feast. It was named after the crew's celebration when the first supply ship arrived from Earth, two years after the settlers had gone to Mars.

It was complicated to get from Earth to Mars because the planets orbited the sun at different speeds. But once every twenty-six Earth months, there was something called a close approach—when Mars was closest to Earth—and that's when the trip was the shortest.

When I walked into the mess hall, the table was groaning with food. Salty Bill had outdone himself. There was pizza made from real flour, and fresh tortillas with rice and beans, and creamy macaroni and cheese. Lime gelatin with strawberries, fruit punch, and mandarin oranges (my favorite).

"Well," Sai said, "I would say that was a successful resupply."

"They sent me plenty of salt," Salty Bill said.

"They forgot a few things from my list," Meems said.

"Ours, too!" Vera said. "Why didn't they send any makeup? We asked for black eyeliner and mascara."

"And blue eye shadow!" Flossy added.

"You don't need makeup," Meems said. "You're both beautiful."

"That's not the point!" Vera said. "We wanted to *try* it!"

I sympathized with them. There were things I wished Earth would send but never did.

"Why don't they ever send cats?" I asked.

"Because you need a human to transport a cat, and they suspended the Nanny Program a few years after the troubles on Earth began," Sai explained.

"Such a shame," Phinneus said, shaking his head.

The Nanny Program was an international project to encourage young people to settle on Mars. They could be scientists or engineers or cooks or plumbers or a dozen other things. They just had to have some talent that was useful in a settlement. The catch was that each person, or "nanny," had to bring an orphaned baby and take care of it on the journey. Babies did surprisingly well in space. Once on Mars, the nanny dropped the baby off at the host country settlement, then went on to their own country.

"Lissa was my nanny, right?" Flossy asked.

Sai looked down at the table. "Yes."

"I'll never forget that poor nanny who brought Vera up," Meems said, and laughed. "He walked off the ship, passed me the baby, and asked where the train was. He didn't even want to stay for supper. He looked shell-shocked."

"Why?" Vera asked.

"Apparently, you cried nonstop," Meems replied.

"What about me? What kind of baby was I?" I asked.

"Probably an annoying one," Trey said.

"Trey!" Meems chastised.

"Sorry," he muttered, but he didn't sound very sorry.

Phinneus patted my arm reassuringly. "You were a good baby," he said with a smile.

"What does a good baby do anyway?" Flossy asked.

"Sleeps, of course," Meems said.

All the grown-ups seemed to think this was hilarious and laughed.

"Time for dessert," Salty Bill announced.

For dessert, there was banana pudding and my favorite—chocolate cake.

When we were finished eating, we pulled out a board game. But after a few minutes, Flossy announced that she was bored.

"I'm tired of board games! Let's dance!" she said.

"Dance?" Sai asked.

"Earth dancing is so fun! There are so many different styles!" Flossy insisted, and started listing them. "The Charleston, the moonwalk, the Macarena!"

"You should show them your moves, Jelly," Eliana said, elbowing her husband.

"Not without you, Peanut Butter," he said, holding his hand out to her.

She took it and said, "We need something to dance to."

Meems went over and fiddled with the digi-player. A moment later, the soft sounds of an old Earth song filled the room.

The pair clasped hands and glided smoothly together around the room.

"That's a waltz!" Flossy declared. "Oh, it's so romantic."

I didn't know about romantic.

But at least the cake was delicious.

Hours later, I was still thinking about cake. Probably because I had woken up and couldn't fall back asleep. Albie was snoring his head off.

I grabbed my new quilt and made my way through the dim corridor. As I passed the mess hall, I decided I deserved a treat for my interrupted sleep and stopped in the kitchen. I cut myself a big slice of chocolate cake and took it upstairs to the COR for a midnight snack.

When I reached the top of the stairs, I was surprised to see that the lights were on.

Sai was sitting at the desk, staring at the bright digi-slate, when I crept into the room. I peeked over his shoulder.

DATE: 5.6.2091
FROM: US Terrestrial Command
TO: CDR Dexter
MESSAGE: Ongoing Hostilities

Please be advised that hostilities in Antarctica are ongoing.

US Terrestrial Command
United States

He turned to me. "It's rude to snoop. What are you doing here?" he asked.

"Albie's snoring again," I said.

"Humph," he said.

"What's 'hostilities' mean?" I asked, nodding at the screen.

"Fighting."

"Who's fighting?"

"More like who isn't?" he said. "France. China. Russia. Japan, I think. Probably a few more."

"What are they fighting over?"

"Rare Earth elements, I believe. A port, too, or maybe shipping lanes," Sai said, and shook his head. "It's been going on so long, I'm afraid I've lost track."

"Who was my nanny?" I asked.

"Her name was Alexandra. She was Russian," Sai said. "Everyone called her Sasha."

"What did she do?"

"She was a biologist."

"Do you have any pictures of her?" I asked.

"Perhaps," he said, and turned to the digi-slate.

He tapped around, scrolling through various folders.

"Ah, this is the one," he said, clicking.

The people in the digi-pic were young adults. They were wearing shirts that said "I brought a baby to Mars, and all I got was this lousy T-shirt."

"Which one is she?" I asked.

He pointed out a dark-haired girl. "That's Sasha."

"Who are the rest?"

His finger traced across the screen. "That's Helmi. Madeleine. Zhang." He hesitated over the last person. "And that was our Lissa."

I stared at the dark-eyed young woman with the smiling face. She looked bubbly. Funny. Warm.

"She looks so happy," I said.

"She was a bright light," he said, and a look of deep sadness crossed his face.

He clicked the picture shut and turned to me, his eyes resting on my cake.

"Did Salty Bill say you could have that?" he asked.

"He was asleep, so I couldn't ask."

He raised an eyebrow. "Well, if you share it with me, I'll forget to tell him you ate it."

I handed him the fork.

DATE: 5.8.2091
FROM: CDR Dexter
TO: US Terrestrial Command
MESSAGE: Situation Report

We are missing the following requested items from the supply ship:

- Rosemary spice
- Fever/pain reliever
- Socket wrench
- Replacement parts for the rover, as listed on attached document
- Moisturizing skin cream
- Blue eye shadow, mascara, and black eyeliner (for the teenagers)

Sai Dexter, COMMANDER
Expeditionary & Settlement Team
United States Territory, Mars

Chapter Twelve

FAMILY NAME

I stared at the glowing digi-slate as I sat at the desk in the COR.

Meems always made us kids write thank-you transmissions for the supplies from Earth. She said it was good manners. I hated it. It was awkward writing to people you'd never met. But there was no getting out of it.

> Dear Earth Command,
>
> Thanks for the supplies. Salty Bill made chocolate cake. It was delicious. Do you think you could send some kittens? Please thank the children at Lincoln Elementary for the quilt. It's warm.

The signature part of the letter was always a bit confusing. I knew that on Earth, people had two names—a first and a last one. Meems explained that the last name indicated your family. But here on Mars, we children only had first names. Part of me thought having a family name would be nice.

In the end, I signed it the same as always:

Your friend,
Bell

After I was done, I clicked Send. The supper bell rang softly in the distance. Time to go.

I made my way down the stairs, and as I neared the bottom, I heard Phinneus and Sai arguing. Loudly.

"You know my feelings on this, Sai," Phinneus said.

"How could I not?" Sai replied sarcastically. "You won't stop telling me I'm wrong."

"It's shortsighted and foolish!" Phinneus shouted.

This was shocking. I'd never even heard Phinneus raise his voice, let alone shout.

"Nonsense."

"You're letting your emotions get in the way," Phinneus said.

"It has nothing to do with emotions. It's what's best for the children."

"They are *all our* children, Sairam," Phinneus insisted. "I love them, too. I want them to lead happy, fulfilling lives. They can't do that confined here. This wasn't meant to be a prison!"

"We are not going to discuss this again!" Sai said, cutting him off.

Then there was the sound of feet walking fast down the corridor. A moment later, I heard Phinneus and his cane slowly following the same way.

I waited a few minutes, then went to the mess hall. Everyone was already eating. I watched as Phinneus and Sai calmly discussed which vegetables to put on rotation. You wouldn't have known that they'd just been at each other's throats.

Eliana was giving us lessons today. She was my favorite teacher because she was fun. She'd taught us how to drive the rover and make rockets. Lately, she'd been teaching us to speak French. Sai didn't approve of this, but she said knowing different languages was important.

"All right," Eliana said. "Let's run through our basic phrases. Repeat after me."

Bonjour. (Hello.)

Je voudrais de l'eau. (I would like some water.)

Où sont les toilettes? (Where are the toilets?)

Vera made an annoyed noise. "I don't know why we have to learn French. French people aren't very nice, you know."

"I think you have the wrong idea about them," Eliana said.

"I remember them chasing us with those weapons," Vera muttered under her breath.

Before anyone could respond, the emergency alarm started blaring.

"Again?" I said.

We followed the sound to the mess hall. Sai was right behind us, which meant this was a real emergency.

"Who pushed the alarm?" he demanded as everyone else rushed in. He swiftly disabled it.

"I did!" Salty Bill shouted, waving a spatula.

"Fire?"

He shook his head wildly. He looked terrified.

"Then what?" Sai demanded.

"It—it—it's in there!" he said, pointing his shaking spatula toward the storage closet.

It?

I turned to the rest of the kids and silently mouthed, "Alien?"

Trey's eyes widened, Albie shook his head, and Flossy's mouth opened into an O. Even Vera seemed a little scared.

But Sai just grabbed a plastic broom that was leaning against a wall (what good was a plastic broom?!) and walked into the large closet. A moment later, we heard him yelp.

"Sai?" Darby hollered, and ran in after him. He grabbed Salty Bill's prized rolling pin. It was made of real Earth wood and was solid.

We waited breathlessly.

"Are you kidding me!" Darby shouted.

That was it. As if on cue, we crowded into the storage closet like an invading army. I struggled to get a good look. Nothing seemed out of place.

"Over there," Sai said, pointing to a counter where a plate of muffins was cooling on a rack.

A small, furry creature with a long tail and whiskers was nibbling on a muffin.

"I thought aliens would be bigger," Vera said, clearly unimpressed.

"That's not an alien," Sai said.

"It's a mouse!" I exclaimed. "A real, live Earth mouse!"

"Awww, it's so cute!" Flossy cried.

"But how did it get here?" Albie asked.

"Must have hitched a ride," Eliana said, and chuckled.

"More like an entire family hitched a ride," Darby said, nudging an open bag of flour with his foot. A bunch more mice ran out.

"Can we keep them?" Flossy asked.

"They're little monsters!" Salty Bill shouted. "Look what they did to my muffins! I just baked them!"

"I don't think that's a good idea," Eliana began. "Mice eat through wiring."

"Just one mouse?" Flossy wheedled, her brown eyes wide. "Pleeeease?"

Meems's face softened. No one could resist Flossy.

"One mouse," Meems agreed. "You'll have to put it in a box with a lid and air holes, to keep Leo away from it."

"Which one?" I asked.

The mice raced madly around the floor.

Sai snorted. "Whichever one you can catch."

Eliana helped us design a plastic habitat for our new pet. It had podlike buildings and tubes for the mouse to run around in. We lined it with torn-up algae paper (Phinneus's suggestion) and a little bowl of water. It looked like a mini Mars settlement, fit for a mouse.

That turned out to be the easy part. The hard part was coming up with a name we could all agree on. We'd been debating names for the last hour. Nobody was happy with any of them, although Trey was pushing hard for John Glenn.

"I've got it! I've got it!" Flossy said, clapping her hands. "Let's name him Muffin!"

"Muffin?" Trey asked.

"We found him eating the muffins!" Flossy insisted.

We all stared at the mouse. With its soft-looking fur and twitching whiskers, the name fit perfectly. Except something was missing.

"We need to give him a last name, too," I said.

"A last name?" Flossy asked.

"He needs a last name so that he knows he's part of our family."

"That sounds like a dumb—" Trey started to say, but Flossy elbowed him.

"What were you thinking, Bell?" Albie asked me.

I stared at the mouse's twitching nose. "What if we called him Muffin of Mars?"

"Simple," Flossy said. "I love it!"

Everyone nodded.

"Welcome to the American settlement, Muffin of Mars," I whispered.

Chapter Thirteen

LOVE AND ATTENTION

One inhabitant of our settlement wasn't happy about Muffin.

Leo.

He prowled around Muffin's habitat like the mouse was a piece of chocolate cake he couldn't wait to taste. After he almost knocked the habitat off the table in the recreation room, we decided to move it somewhere with less cat traffic: the algae farm.

Phinneus was delighted to have the mouse there. He even made special peanut-butter algae mouse treats.

"You like these treats, don't you, darling?" he crooned as he fed the mouse. I think he loved Muffin even more than we kids did.

"He's a good mouse," I said.

"*He?*" he asked. "That's a female."

"Oh," I said. "How can you tell?"

"Grow up on a farm, and you'll learn fast," he said with a wry look.

"Do you think we should have saved two mice?" I asked him. "Won't Muffin get lonely without a friend? He— I mean *she*—doesn't have anyone to play with."

Kind of like me these days.

"Ah, I see," he said, and gave me a knowing look. "We'll just have to give her a lot of love and attention, then, right?"

"Right," I said.

We watched Muffin scratch at the edges of the walls of the habitat as if trying to get out.

"Poor thing wants her freedom," Phinneus observed.

"But it's not safe outside for her," I said.

He gave me a long look.

"I suppose," he said. "But living in a cage is no kind of life, even for a mouse."

·ö·

Flossy poked her head through my door. "Pssst! Come to our room!"

I looked up from my book. I'd been reading about mice.

"No way," I said. "Last time I did that, I ended up in a sling."

"Oh, come on, silly. This is about Meems's birthday. It's perfectly safe!"

"Okay," I said. "But if any of you talk about stealing a rover, I'm leaving."

When I got to the older kids' room, she shut the door. Albie and Trey and Vera were already there.

"It's Meems's birthday next week," Flossy said. "We're going to throw her a surprise party!"

"We are?" I asked.

"Yes! I have it all figured out!" she said. "And you're going to help!"

·ö·

The next morning, I nosed around the shelves in Sai's workshop. We needed duct tape to hang the decorations on the walls. Flossy figured I could grab a roll on my dust rounds. When I'd left the mess hall, Sai was still eating breakfast.

The duct tape wasn't in the usual bin, so I started to dig around in the supplies. Finding where Sai had hidden it didn't take long; it was next to a box marked "Sai—Personal." I was curious, so I opened it.

The box was full of random things. A pirate hat. A folded piece of paper that said *Je t'aime*. A red T-shirt with the words "We Did It!" And a dry, crisp-looking plant. It was purple and looked like an Earth flower. When I lifted it to my nose, it still held a faint perfume.

At the bottom of the box was an award of some kind.

1ST PLACE AWARD

1st

**FIRST ANNUAL
MARS HALLOWEEN PARTY
BEST COSTUME: SAI
COUNTRY: USA**

I heard footsteps coming down the hall, so I shoved everything into the box and pushed it back. Then I rushed to the wall where the filter was and pretended to empty the dust.

Sai stopped short when he saw me. "Well, you got an early start today."

I grinned. "Yep! Already done!"

When I went to walk past him with my bucket, his hand came down on my shoulder. Luckily, it was my good one.

"I don't recall giving you that duct tape," he said.

Aw, dust it.

"What are you up to?" he asked.

"Nothing," I said.

He raised an eyebrow. "Bell."

"We're throwing a surprise birthday party for Meems and need tape to hang the decorations," I said in a rush.

"I see." He studied me. "In that case, you may take the duct tape."

"Thanks," I said.

"By the way, I'm looking forward to trying your carrot cake," he said, and turned away.

My mouth dropped open.

Like I said, it was impossible to keep a secret on Mars.

⚙

The night before Meems's birthday, I went up to Salty Bill as he was putting things away in the kitchen.

"Would it be okay if I did some cooking tonight?" I asked. "I just thought I would make some cookies."

He gave me a hard look. Finally, he said, "Make sure you clean up when you're done. I don't want to find a sink full of dishes tomorrow morning."

"Sure, no problem," I told him.

"Also," he said, "use toasted pecans in the batter. That's my trick for a great carrot cake."

I shook my head. Honestly, was there *anyone* Phinneus hadn't told?

Albie offered to help me bake the cake. He was the best cook of all us kids. He patiently walked me through the recipe step-by-step. It was late by the time I'd finished spreading the white icing on the cake. I stood back to admire my work.

"What do you think?" I asked him.

"Hmm," he said. "What if we decorated the top with some more carrots? Stick them in the cake so they look like they're growing out of the icing?"

"Oooh! That's a great idea!" I said. "I'll go grab a few from the farm."

"I'll start cleaning up this mess," he said, looking at the pile of dirty bowls we'd used.

"Okay," I said.

Leo was sniffing and scratching at the door to the algae farm when I arrived.

"Mwar!" he said, which meant *Let me in!* in Cat.

"Sorry, Leo," I told him. "You can't eat Muffin."

I opened the door and slid inside, closing it quickly so Leo couldn't follow. That didn't stop him from yowling.

A familiar sight greeted me: Phinneus was asleep at the table, his head pillowed on his arms. Across from him, Muffin darted around her habitat.

I headed back to get the carrots. The tops were tall and fuzzy and green. I pulled one up from the container. It was fat and perfect.

In short order, I'd harvested my carrots. I was carrying them out when I paused by the table where Phinneus was sleeping.

"Did you tell every single person in the settlement that I was making this cake for Meems?" I asked him.

Phinneus slept on.

"It's supposed to be a surprise," I said. "Please tell me you didn't tell Meems."

He didn't speak.

Across from him, Muffin started running madly on the wheel we'd made for her habitat. The wheel rattled noisily, but Phinneus slept on.

It was odd.

"Phinneus," I said, shaking him gently, and then froze.

Because something was very wrong. His body was so still. Too still. I leaned closer and touched his chest to see if it was moving.

It wasn't.

That's when I started screaming.

DATE: 6.2.2091
FROM: CDR Dexter
TO: US Terrestrial Command
MESSAGE: Situation Report

Yesterday at approximately 22:05 hours, Mission Specialist Phinneus Peck was found unresponsive in the algae farm. Attempts to resuscitate him were unsuccessful. He was declared deceased at 22:44 hours.

Please notify next of kin.

Sai Dexter, COMMANDER
Expeditionary & Settlement Team
United States Territory, Mars

Chapter Fourteen

CAKE

Instead of a birthday party, there was a funeral.

We put on environmental suits and climbed to the surface. It was a shockingly beautiful day. The sky was clear and light. Albie and Sai carried the bag with Phinneus's body to the little graveyard. They buried him in the dusty red Martian soil, wrapped in his favorite thing—a thick piece of algae paper.

"You were our teammate, our companion, our family. We will miss you, Phinneus," Sai said, his voice crackling over my headset.

I looked at Meems. Tears were running down her face, the same way they were running down mine.

"Rest now, old friend," Sai said. "You've earned it."

Then we piled rocks on top of the grave, and everyone cried.

After the burial, we gathered in the mess hall to have lunch. I couldn't stop looking at Phinneus's empty chair, remembering what had happened yesterday. It was a fuzzy blur, like a digi-reel on fast-forward, all jumbled images. Sai and Eliana running into the algae farm. Phinneus's still body. The look of horror on Sai's face. Eliana hitting the alarm. Meems running in with her bag. Her holding my shoulders and telling me I had non-med shock, then giving me a shot in the arm as I cried and cried and cried. How everything seemed to drift away into darkness.

Phinneus was dead.

"Are you okay?" Flossy asked me from across the table.

I shook my head. How could I possibly be okay when Phinneus was dead? I would never be able to talk to him again. Never hear his laugh. He was gone, and nothing would ever be the same.

After Meems's shot yesterday, I slept for a while. When I woke up, I was back in my own bed. For a moment, I thought maybe it had all been a bad dream. But then I saw Albie's tearstained face and knew it had actually happened.

Something else was bothering me, too. Meems said Phinneus had died from a heart attack. She said it was typical for old people. I know she thought she was being reassuring, but I was horrified. Because when I looked at the grown-ups, all I could see was gray hair and wrinkles.

Under the lunch table, I felt fur brush my ankle and looked down at Leo.

"Meow," he said. He looked sad, too.

I couldn't help but wonder if Leo had known all along. Was that why he had been scratching at the door? Had he been trying to save Phinneus?

At the far end of the table, Sai took a deep breath. "I've informed Command of Phinneus's death. They'll notify his next of kin."

"Is his brother still alive?" Eliana asked.

"He died last year," Meems said. "But there's a nephew, I believe. I'll send a personal condolence message from all of us."

That sounded nice, but who would send a condolence message to *us*? Who would tell us how sorry they were that we'd lost a member of our family? Because that's what Phinneus had been—family.

A wave of sadness washed over me.

Darby laughed. "Do you remember the time Phinneus thought he had discovered a new species?"

Salty Bill chuckled. "I'd nearly forgotten about that."

"What happened?" Flossy asked.

Meems turned to me with a smile. "He'd gone outside and collected a sample of something. He was convinced it was some new organism."

Darby picked up the story. "He put it in a dish, and

lo and behold, something grew from the sample. He was so excited!"

"When he studied his new species, he realized it was just a, ahem, booger," Meems said.

"A booger?" I asked.

"Yes," Meems said. "One of you children had stuck a booger in the sample."

"Whose was it?" I asked.

"Put it this way: he told us he would name this new organism *T. vera*," Meems said.

Vera reddened, and everybody laughed.

Around the room it went. One story after another. And with each story, my heart felt a little lighter.

I had so many favorite memories of Phinneus. It was hard to pick just one. But I think it was the time he'd taught me how to plant seeds. Dig a hole, drop the seed, cover it with soil, add a little water, and wait. I still remembered my amazement when the green sprouts had finally burst through the soil.

Flossy walked out of the kitchen, carrying the cake.

"Happy birthday, Meems," she said with a sad smile. "We were going to throw you a surprise party, but ..."

"It's carrot cake," Albie said. "It was Bell's idea."

"Oh, Bell," Meems said, looking teary-eyed. "Thank you."

Flossy sliced the cake and passed plates down the table. But I just stared at my piece.

"Aren't you going to eat it?" Salty Bill asked me.

"It feels bad eating cake when Phinneus isn't here," I whispered.

"He'd want you to enjoy it," he said gruffly. "He was never one to waste a piece of cake."

That made me smile because it was true.

So I ate my slice.

·ờ·

Phinneus was gone, but life went on in the settlement.

It was shocking how the loss of a single person had affected our little world. Even though Phinneus had been meticulous about making notes in the Record, there were many things that only he knew. When Phinneus had died, he had taken all his experience with him.

Albie, who had picked up the algae farm in addition to his other responsibilities, was frustrated. One day, he told me a batch of algae had turned out bad.

"I don't know where anything is," he confessed. "I can't find the fertilizer for the beets."

"It's probably in the cabinet over the sink," I said.

"And there's a leak in the container growing the spinach. I can't figure out what's causing it."

"It's probably the roots," I told him. "They can clog things and cause a backup."

Albie looked surprised. "How do you know all this?"

"I just remember Phinneus telling me."

"Can you help me figure things out?" he asked.

I hadn't been in the algae farm since Phinneus died.

Albie must have seen something on my face, because he said, "That was dumb of me. Forget I even asked."

"No, it's okay," I told him. "I'll come help."

It felt wrong to be back in the algae farm.

Everywhere I looked, there were living things. Algae, vegetables, fruit. All so green and growing, coaxed to life and nurtured by Phinneus. But he was gone. It was so unfair. I'd never had a chance to tell him good-bye. Even a plant said farewell in its own way. It sagged, leaves falling off, one by one, until finally there was nothing left but a lonely, bare stem.

Remember me, it whispered.

"This place is kind of confusing." Albie scratched his head as if he didn't know where to start.

Stuff was piled randomly on shelves—seeds and tools and fertilizers and hydroponic parts. Phinneus wasn't organized. In fact, he was pretty much the opposite of Sai, with his perfectly lined-up bins.

We decided I would label and organize the supplies so the others could find them more easily.

"What's this herb? It doesn't taste very good," Albie said, holding out a sprig of green.

"It's catnip," I said.

"Oh," he said, and made a face.

For the first time in days, I laughed.

After that, we decided it was probably a good idea to label the plants, too.

Chapter Fifteen

STORM

S ai was barking orders when we walked into breakfast the next morning.

"And shut down noncritical areas so we can preserve power," he told Eliana.

She nodded and hurried off, her husband following her.

"What's going on?" Albie asked Sai.

Sai wasn't his usually composed self. He looked stressed.

"I received a weather report during the night," he said. "A dust storm is scheduled to hit."

The problem with dust storms was that they kicked up dust in the air, which blocked the sunlight. The majority of our power was solar, so we would have to rely much more on batteries.

"When?" I asked Sai.

"In about forty-eight hours."

·✵·

The dust storm began.

As the days passed, it seemed to get denser much faster than was typical. When I went up to the COR in the middle of the afternoon a few days later, the sky was a dusty haze, like twilight. It was eerie.

And the storm lingered. Usually a dust storm lasted for a few days. But after many weeks, there was still no end in sight.

At supper that night, Sai gave us the bad news.

"I just heard from Command. The storm is officially a Big One," he said.

Every decade or so there was a dust storm that covered the entire planet. This global dust storm was known as a Big One. It was impossible to predict how long it would last.

But that wasn't the only bad news.

Something had happened to our batteries—a bunch weren't working—so energy had to be strictly rationed. Sai had ordered the heat to be turned lower, and there were no hot showers.

So we bundled up in our warmest thermal suits and shivered in the shower.

We kids spent most of our time in the mess hall. I had pulled out a puzzle and spread it on the floor to piece together. It was of Earth—all the countries and the great oceans.

"How long is this storm going to last?" Flossy asked, struggling with two plastic sticks and a ball of yarn. Meems had been teaching her how to knit.

"It's hard to say," Meems said.

"I can't wait to wash my hair in hot water," Vera said. It was greasy, just like mine.

"Do they have dust storms on Earth?" Trey asked Meems from where he sat on the floor.

He was working on the puzzle with me. Since the dust storm had arrived, it was as if a truce had been called.

"Yes," she said. "But Earth storms are generally wind and water. They're called hurricanes."

Sometimes when the grown-ups talked about life on Earth, it felt like they were remembering dreams. Water falling from the sky. Earth animals flying. Places called libraries, where you could simply walk in and take books home. It all seemed so fantastic.

"I remember a bad storm that just about destroyed my grandfather's little house in the Florida Keys," Meems said. "The wind blew the water horizontally, and we couldn't figure out where the leaks were. What a mess that was! Had to gut the entire house."

Salty Bill wandered out of the kitchen in his apron to check on our progress. "How is it going?" he asked.

"Not very well," I said.

I'd been trying to figure out where to put my piece for half an hour. We had finished the edges and parts of some countries, but only Antarctica was complete. How strange that this place was the cause of so much trouble.

I held out my piece. "I can't figure out where it goes."

Salty Bill got down on his knees and studied the puzzle.

"I think that's the top of Maine," he told me.

I clicked it down, and it fit. "Thanks!"

He winked. "You know, the best lobster I ever had in my life was in Maine."

Vera looked disgusted. "Lobster? You ate a lobster? How could you? They're so cute!"

Salty Bill snorted. "Real lobsters are not cute. But they sure are tasty. Especially with drawn butter and lemon. Best meal of my life."

At the table, Meems leaned forward. "I had the best meal of my life in Provence. Roast chicken, green beans, and grilled potatoes. Simple, yet perfect somehow."

"Cute little chickens and lobsters? This is why I'm happy to live on Mars. I don't know how you could ever eat Earth animals," Vera said, and I had to agree.

"Where's Provence?" Flossy asked.

"In southern France," Meems said. "There are fields of purple lavender. I still remember the smell."

"That sounds so romantic," Flossy said.

"France is a beautiful country," Meems agreed.

"But I don't understand. The French people here are dangerous. They chased us!" I said.

Salty Bill and Meems shared a long look.

Finally, she said, "Countries fight for different reasons. For instance, the United States fought Great Britain during the Revolutionary War but came to their aid during World War Two. It's complicated."

As usual, Vera had the last word.

"You know what's not complicated?" she said. "Eating cute lobsters. It's just wrong."

DATE: 7.16.2091
FROM: CDR Dexter
TO: US Terrestrial Command
MESSAGE: Situation Report

The global dust storm is ongoing. We have instituted standard protocols. Please advise on forecasted duration of storm.

Sai Dexter, COMMANDER
Expeditionary & Settlement Team
United States Territory, Mars

Chapter Sixteen

DUST

The first hint that something was wrong was a cough.

We were having supper—a hearty stew with pota-toes and onions—when Eliana started coughing. It was a deep, hacking cough that sounded terrible.

"Are you okay, Peanut Butter?" Darby asked.

Her smile was strained. "It's just a little cough, Jelly."

By the next day, Eliana was in bed. Sick.

"I think it's dust cough," Meems told Sai. "Even though she's in the enviro suit when she goes topside, she has some exposure when she takes it off. Especially with the amount of dust in the atmosphere now."

There was a vacuum room that sucked dust off the enviro suits when you came in, but the dust was so fine, some still made it through. It was like a thin coat of flour. Getting rid of the stuff was nearly impossible.

"Will she be okay?" Sai asked.

"With some rest and steroids, she should get better," Meems said. "She can't go up top anymore."

But Eliana didn't get better. If anything, she got worse. Even more worrying was that Meems had started to cough, too, and was in bed. Now they both had dust cough.

"Maybe the dust filters are backed up," Darby suggested. He looked tired; he'd been up all night, taking care of his sick wife.

"Have you been emptying the dust filters completely?" Sai asked me with a skeptical look.

"Yes," I told him.

"I think we'll join you on your rounds this morning," he told me.

They watched as I emptied the filters. By the time I finished, I had a bucket of dust.

Darby rubbed his chin. "That's a normal amount of dust. I suppose there could be a leak in one of the air ducts."

"What do you suggest?" Sai asked.

"I can send Pup to look at each section. See if there are any cracks."

Pup had a digi-cam and could fit in tight spaces.

"Might as well get started," Sai said.

Inspecting the ductwork was slow going. Pup only had so much battery power, so he had to take frequent breaks to recharge. It was nearly midnight when Darby and Albie walked into the mess hall. Trey and I were still awake and working on the puzzle. We'd finished most of Europe.

"Well?" Trey asked.

"Nothing," Albie said.

Darby's face was gray with fatigue. "Well, I don't know about you boys, but I'm going to bed."

⚙

The next morning at breakfast, it was just us kids and Sai and Salty Bill. Darby was exhausted and sleeping in.

Salty Bill had made muffins with chocolate bits. They were delicious.

Sai was ignoring his muffin; he was poring over schematics of the settlement.

Vera screwed up her face. "What if the dust is getting in here like during the hurricane?"

She'd washed her hair, but now instead of being greasy, it looked just ratty. I guess cold water didn't get the dirt out.

Sai looked curious. "What's this?"

"Meems said rain blew horizontally during a bad hurricane and got through tiny cracks, so there were leaks in her grandfather's house in Florida," she said. "Maybe the dust is getting in cracks somewhere?"

Albie looked excited. "It could be coming in through the communications room."

"Definitely a possibility," Sai conceded. "I suppose we ought to investigate the roof. We'll need a few hands. At least two people to hold the ladder steady and someone to climb up."

"I'll do it," Albie said.

Sai hesitated. "You may be too big to climb on the roof. It will probably support your weight, but if there's any weakness, now's not the time to stress it."

"Oh," Albie said, and looked down.

"I can do it," Trey offered, and I could hear the hopeful note in his voice.

Sai regarded him steadily. "All right."

Trey flushed with happiness.

"I'll still need another hand to help with the ladder," Sai said.

"I'm taking care of Meems," Flossy said.

Vera groaned dramatically. "Guess it's me. Oh well, it's not like my hair can actually get any worse."

"I found a small crack!" Trey announced at supper.

He was so excited, he was practically bouncing in his chair.

"Where was it?" I asked.

"Near the base where the supply ship docks," he said. "Sai said it was probably caused by the pressure of the ship docking."

Albie looked skeptical. "But that crack just went into a support piece. It didn't lead to any vents."

"It was still a good find," Trey insisted.

"Sure," Albie agreed. "We'll patch it up tomorrow."

Trey preened.

"So we still don't know how the dust is getting in?" Flossy asked.

"Pretty much," Vera said. "And now my hair looks like a flat, greasy helmet."

Salty Bill leaned out of the kitchen and looked around the room.

"Where is everyone?" he demanded. His voice sounded hoarse.

"I took Meems and Darby and Eliana some soup earlier," Flossy said.

"What about Sai?" Salty Bill asked.

"He wanted to look at schematics of the settlement," Albie told him. "He'll get himself something to eat later."

"Well, I'm closing the kitchen. I think I'm coming down with a cold," Salty Bill said.

The next morning when we went to the mess hall, none of the grown-ups showed up. Not even Salty Bill.

When they didn't appear at supper, we really started to panic.

Chapter Seventeen
PLEASE ADVISE

The sound of coughing echoed up and down the corridors. All the grown-ups were sick.

In a heartbeat, life had changed. Or maybe it had stopped. Like a digi-reel frozen halfway through a scene. Overnight, it was up to us kids to take care of the settlement: cooking, dust duty, repairs, and a hundred other things. It was never-ending.

By some unspoken agreement, Flossy had taken charge. It didn't matter that Albie was older; she knew the most about running the settlement after being Sai's apprentice. It soon became apparent why he had chosen her first: she was great at organizing. With the same enthusiasm and attention to detail she had when making clothes, she kept the settlement running. She could see the big picture of what needed to be done. And she somehow got us to do the work without fighting.

I spent most of my time helping Albie make meals and

nurse the grown-ups. Flossy insisted that we clean our hands with a sanitizing spray every time we left one of the grown-ups' bedrooms. She was worried that we would get sick, too. I was more worried about my skin: the sanitizing spray was harsh, and I had dry, red patches all over my hands from using it.

"Take this to Meems," Albie told me, spooning some soup into a bowl. "When you're done, come and get Sai's. I'll do Darby and Eliana and Salty Bill."

The grown-ups were getting sicker. I'd never seen anyone this ill. Sure, the occasional cold made its way around the settlement, but it was usually just a sore throat and a stuffy nose.

"Albie, is it normal for everyone to get sick at the same time?"

"I don't think so," he said, and his shoulders drooped.

I carried the tray to Meems's room. I could hear her coughing from behind the door.

"Meems?" I called. "I brought you some lunch."

"Come in," she said, her voice a croak.

When I opened the door, I saw that Meems was in bed, the covers tucked up to her chin. Her short, fuzzy gray hair was slick with sweat, and her face was pale. Meems shivered even though she was under a pile of blankets. Now she seemed fragile, like she could crumple and blow away.

"How do you feel?" I asked her.

"I think I have a fever again," she said. "Can you give me some more of the painkiller, Kitten?"

I put the soup down, got the bottle on the table, and shook out two tablets. Then I propped her up with pillows and handed her the medicine and water. Our roles were reversed: I was taking care of her like she was a child.

She settled back with a sigh. "How are the others doing?"

"Eliana's coughing is getting worse," I said. "And Flossy said Salty Bill is coughing really bad and has a fever, too. Same with Sai."

"They both have fevers?"

I nodded.

A puzzled look crossed her face. "This just doesn't seem like dust cough."

A blur of fur bounded into the room. Leo. He did a slow patrol of the room, sniffing here and there.

"He's hunting for mice," I told Meems.

She stared at Leo.

"Lice," she whispered.

"Leo has lice?" I asked.

She drew a deep breath and coughed. "They were stowaways. Like the lice."

"Who were?"

Her eyes met mine.

"The mice," she whispered. "It's the mice."

·❂·

While the mouse disease didn't affect us kids, the grown-ups didn't have any resistance to it.

But the worst part was knowing that it wasn't aliens or the other countries that had brought danger to our home: it was something from Earth. What if other threats were lurking in the supplies? Was it even safe to eat the food? Had one of the killer weeds Phinneus had told me about hopped a ride, too? It was terrifying to consider.

The days turned into weeks, and we struggled to keep things going. Albie came to bed late every night. Between cooking and taking care of the grown-ups, he barely slept.

Tonight was no different. He staggered in and collapsed on his bed. For a moment, he just lay there, staring at the ceiling.

"You okay?" I asked him.

"I'm so tired," he said. "Can you stay with Sai tonight? His fever is bad."

"Sure," I said.

"I already gave him medicine. He was asleep a little while ago. Make him drink water if you can."

"Okay."

And then he closed his eyes and started snoring. He hadn't even changed into his pajamas.

Like Albie, Sai was fast asleep, a low light glowing next to his bed. I touched his forehead. It felt hot.

I wandered around, looking at the digi-pics on the wall.

There was Sai as a young boy with an older woman—his

mother?—standing in front of a house with leafy trees. A teenage version of Sai with his arm around another teenage boy, sitting on an Earth car vehicle and grinning at the camera. Another of them as young men in uniform. They were trying to look serious, but Sai was actually cracking a smile. Another digi-pic of the two of them wearing fancy black suits. The other man was kissing a woman in a white dress with some kind of netting on her head.

"Larry," Sai said, his voice anxious. "Where's Larry?"

Who was Larry? There was no Larry in the settlement. I went over to him. "Sai?"

"Larry!" he shouted, trying to sit up.

I didn't know what to do—it was scary. Then he started coughing so hard, he couldn't breathe.

"Sai, you should lie back down," I urged.

But he wouldn't; he just got more agitated. Like Trey when he didn't get his way.

"Larry!" he shouted.

"Please, Sai!"

Then his eyes seemed to focus on me. "There you are," he said.

"I've been here the whole time."

He sagged against the bed. "I've missed you so much, Larry."

"It's Bell, Sai," I told him. "Don't you recognize me?"

"Promise you'll stay, Larry."

My stomach fell. He had no idea who I was.

"Promise me," he said.

"I'll stay," I said. "Now go to sleep."

I watched his chest rise and fall with each slow breath.

⚙

The next morning, I stared at my breakfast. I wasn't hungry; I was too shaken by what had happened with Sai.

"He didn't know you at all?" Flossy asked.

"It was weird. He thought I was someone named Larry."

"Maybe it was the fever," she said, picking up her spoon.

Breakfast was basic: algae porridge. It was bland but filling. Meals were something to be eaten in a hurry now, not lingered over. I missed Salty Bill's cooking. Now I knew why he had been the first person Sai recruited: tasty food definitely helped morale. And our morale needed all the help it could get. Flossy had dark circles under her eyes. Albie was wearing the same clothes he'd had on yesterday. Trey sagged in his chair. Even Vera was too tired to be her usual snarky self.

"The toilet in the grown-ups' wing won't flush," Vera said.

"When did that happen?" Flossy asked.

"This morning," she said.

"I swear this place is held together with duct tape," Flossy said.

She wasn't wrong.

"I'll add it to the list," she said.

Albie suddenly burst into tears.

We were so startled that we just stared at him.

"Albie?" I whispered. "What's wrong?"

But he continued to sob.

"Albie, take a breath," Flossy said in a soothing voice. "Everything's going to be fine—"

"Everything's not going to be fine!" he cried. "We're almost out of pain medicine!"

"We are?" she asked, her voice sharp.

He nodded, his eyes wet with tears.

Flossy swallowed.

Then Albie pulled his ball cap over his eyes and put his head in his arms and cried.

I wanted to cry, too.

·☼·

I helped Flossy put Albie to bed. Vera was waiting for us in the hall when we left the bedroom.

"We have to do something!" she hissed.

"I'm doing everything I can," Flossy protested.

"The grown-ups aren't getting better. We need to send

a message to Earth Command! Tell them we need help! We can't handle this anymore! We're kids!"

Flossy brightened. "That's a good idea."

Vera threw up her hands in frustration. "Of course it's a good idea! I swear I'm the only person on this entire planet with any sense!"

Flossy frowned. "I don't know Sai's log-in password."

"It's taped on a piece of paper under the digi-slate," I told her.

Vera looked impressed. "Why, you little snoop!"

I blushed. I didn't snoop; I just *noticed* things.

"Come on," Vera told me. "I'll send the transmission."

She and I went up to the COR. When she picked up the digi-slate, his log-in was there, scribbled on a piece of paper. It said:

My_Larry

Who was this Larry? Was this the same Larry Sai was talking to during his fever?

I helped her log in. As she wrote the message to Command, I looked outside. The storm was still going on, the sky that strange hazy color.

"Done," Vera said, standing up. "I just sent it. I signed Sai's name so they won't think it's a prank."

Years ago, the older kids had used Sai's password and

sent a message with fart jokes to Earth Command. They hadn't been amused. I didn't think Earth Command had a sense of humor.

"How long until we hear back from them?" I asked.

"It won't take long to reach Earth, but they'll take hours to figure out what to say. No sense waiting."

"Okay," I said, staring at the monitor. "I'll be down in a minute to do the dishes." They'd been piling up.

She nodded and left the room.

Then I sat and logged in to Sai's account. I scrolled through Sai's messages with Earth Command. Once I started reading, I couldn't stop. He worried about everything—from Trey's pimples to the strength of the outside coating of the COR. He ended almost every message with the same phrase: *Please advise.*

Command always responded the same way: we'll send whatever you need on the next supply ship. At first, it struck me as a little cold, but then I realized it was all they could do. They were too far away to actually help. Like the sun in my bedroom, it was all an illusion. The truth was that we were on our own.

And we always had been.

DATE: 8.12.2091
FROM: US Terrestrial Command
TO: CDR Dexter
MESSAGE: Re: Situation Report

We are in receipt of your situation report regarding the current medical status of the adult mission crew members. After consulting with our physicians, we believe they are suffering from the Yermo virus. It originated in mice in Yermo, New California, over two decades ago and spread to humans. The children must have been exposed to it on Earth, which is why they have not fallen ill.

All rodents should be exterminated, as they are disease vectors. In addition, we are dispatching antiviral medication on an expedited supply ship. The children should be treated with the antiviral medication as well, since they may not have full immunity. Yermo virus is fatal without treatment. Due to the launch window, it will reach you in approximately eight months.

Evelyn Morris, COMMANDER
Mars Space Command
United States

Chapter Eighteen

EXTERMINATE

We gathered in the dim light of the COR to stare at the message from Command.

"Eight months?" Albie whispered.

"I figured as much," Flossy said. "We're already past the good launch window."

"What does 'exterminate' mean?" I asked.

"It means 'kill,'" Vera snapped. "Don't you know anything?"

"They want us to kill Muffin?" I asked, horrified.

Vera bit the inside of her cheek and nodded.

This was so wrong! Someone needed to speak up for Muffin! She needed an attorney to plead her case!

"But she's in the habitat now," I said. "She can't get out! She won't hurt anybody!"

"Muffin's carrying the virus," Flossy said. "It's too dangerous for the grown-ups. And us."

"Do you think this is why Phinneus died? From this mouse virus?" Trey asked.

"Maybe. He was doing fine before. The habitat was in the algae farm, too," Albie said.

"Can't we just put Muffin somewhere out of the way? It's not her fault!" I pleaded.

Flossy shook her head slowly.

I thought of Muffin. Her sweet eyes. Her twitchy whiskers.

"Can we at least say good-bye?" I whispered.

Flossy nodded.

We said good-bye to our mouse.

I gave Muffin one of Phinneus's peanut-butter mouse treats. She nibbled it. I think Muffin knew we loved her. At least, I hope she did.

We decided the kindest thing was to just put Muffin in her habitat on the surface of Mars. So Flossy put on her environmental suit and carried the habitat outside. When she returned, her arms were empty.

It was over.

Albie had made one of my favorite meals—Earth flour waffles with syrup. But no one was hungry. Who could possibly eat after something like this?

I couldn't stop myself from asking. Because I had to know.

"Was it bad?" I whispered. "I mean, do you think it hurt her?"

Flossy put her arm around my shoulder. "She just fell asleep. That was it. She didn't feel a thing."

Trey stared at the table; he seemed paralyzed.

But Vera was angry. At the situation. At the universe. At Earth Command.

"Eight months to get a supply ship here!" she ranted. She was so agitated that I swear her bangs were angry, too. "How's that going to help us?"

"It's the normal response," I said quietly.

She whirled on me. "What?"

"I read through Sai's messages to Command," I told her. "It's not their fault. They're too far away to help us."

"Then we have to save ourselves!" Vera said. "Or *we're* going to be exterminated! Someone needs to go to another settlement and get help. Finland's the closest."

"But we're not allowed to—" Albie began to say.

Vera cut him off with a furious scowl. "Don't even!"

"We can't take the *Yellow Submarine*. Its battery is drained already," Trey said.

"Then take the train," Vera said.

"I guess we don't have much of a choice," Flossy said. "I'll go get ready."

"No-no-no-no-no!" Albie shouted, holding his hands out. "You can't go!"

"Why not?" Flossy asked.

"Because you're the only one who knows how to keep this place running!"

"Hey—" Vera started to stay.

"You don't understand! Flossy can't leave!" Albie shouted. He was losing it. Maybe the lack of sleep had finally caught up to him. "I don't want to be in charge! It's too much!"

Flossy looked around at us.

"I'll go," Trey volunteered.

"Great! Good idea! It's settled, then!" Albie said.

Under the table, I saw Trey's leg bouncing furiously, and I knew what it meant because I knew Trey. He was nervous—scared, even. Who wouldn't be?

"I'll go with you," I blurted out.

He turned to me. "You will?"

"Do not go outside without a buddy," I said. "It's a rule, right?"

Trey's eyes flashed with something—relief?—and he grinned.

"Yeah," he said. "It's a rule."

Chapter Nineteen
VANISHED

Trey and I stood in the train. I was holding a glow stick so we could see. At any other time, getting to ride Percy would have been exciting—an adventure. But all I felt was worried and scared. Worried about the grown-ups. And scared for Trey and me. Would these Finnish people help us, or would they chase us with weapons, like the French people had? I was also anxious about basic things. Like, did the Finnish people even speak English? Flossy had coached us on what to say. She told us to keep it simple: tell them that we were from the American settlement and that we desperately needed help. She'd emphasized the "desperate" part.

Trey stared at the control panel and bit his lip.

"Okay, I think I remember Eliana saying to start the engine before releasing the brake. Does that sound right?"

"I think so," I said.

"Here goes," he said, and pushed the power button. The train rumbled to life.

"It worked!" Trey said, turning to me with a big grin on his face.

"Good job," I told him.

And then we were moving.

The train rocked as it trundled along the track. Trey drove while I sat on one of the benches behind him, remembering. We'd spent so much time talking about Percy, about where we would go if we ever got to drive the train ourselves. He'd always wanted to go to the Russian settlement, and I'd always wanted to go where he went.

Perhaps twenty minutes had passed when I saw a bright light. It was illuminating a platform, and there was a blue-and-white flag hanging above a door. Trey pumped the brakes, pulling alongside the platform. The train slowed, finally jerking to a stop.

Neither of us moved to leave.

"Do you think the Finnish people will be nicer than the French?" I asked.

"I hope so," Trey said. "Come on."

We stepped onto the platform and walked up to the door. Trey knocked, but no one answered.

"Maybe they can't hear us?" he said.

"Should we just walk in?"

"Don't have much of a choice," he said, and tugged

on the door, sliding it open. It was dark ahead, so Trey clicked on a glow stick. As we walked in, the door slid closed with a heavy thud.

Inside, it was cold and the air smelled different—a woodsy Earth scent.

We continued on until we reached a room. Trey found the light switch and clicked it on.

"Whoa," I whispered.

Everywhere I looked, there was color. The walls were painted bright yellow and blue with crazy geometric designs. The couch cushions were red and purple. There was a fluffy orange rug. It was like someone had melted crayons and thrown them all around the room.

Then there was the odd table. It was large and rectangular. Strung vertically across the middle of it was a net. Two oddly shaped plates lay on the table. They had handles.

Where were the chairs? Did they eat standing up? Was it some Finnish thing?

"Hello!" Trey called in a loud voice. "We're from the American territory, and we need help!"

Everything was still and quiet.

"Anyone here?" he called.

But no one answered. It was unsettling.

"Where is everyone?" I whispered.

Trey looked equally disturbed. "I don't know. I guess we should look around."

"Let's stick together," I said.

"Good idea," he agreed quickly.

·ọ·

We walked down the silent corridors, opening doors and peeking in rooms. But it soon became clear why no one had greeted us: there was no one here.

The settlement had been abandoned.

"This is spooky," I said.

"Yeah," Trey agreed.

I felt like a detective in a digi-reel trying to figure out what had happened. Where had they gone? The inhabitants had left clues in the form of neatly made beds and folded clothes. Everything seemed tidy and organized, as if they hadn't left in a hurry.

The kitchen was bigger than ours and gleaming white. There were notes posted to the walls in a language I couldn't read. It definitely wasn't French. One of them read *Puhdista astiat!*

The storage units had some foods I didn't recognize: a strange-smelling dark brown bread and a jar of small black candies. I popped one into my mouth. And promptly spit it out. It didn't taste like candy: it was salty.

But a delicious scent lingered in the air, one I did recognize.

"Do you smell that?" I asked Trey.

"What?"

"Chocolate cake!" I told him. "Someone baked a cake recently."

We opened food storage units, looking for the cake, but there was none in sight. However, we found something far more interesting: a bowl of white oval objects.

"What are those?" Trey asked.

"I think they're eggs!" I told him. "From Earth chickens."

His eyes widened. "There's an Earth chicken on Mars?"

And we made another discovery: kids lived in this settlement. Or had lived here. There were toys. Stuffed animals and child-sized shoes. One kid's bedroom was cat-themed. Posters and drawings of cats were taped to the wall. Even the bedspread had a big grinning orange cat on it, talking about eating something called lasagna. This kid was obsessed with cats. I kind of wanted to meet this person.

After we'd checked all the rooms underground, we climbed upstairs to their communications and observations room. It was empty as well.

There was no sign of the people who lived here.

"It's like they just vanished," Trey said, shaking his head.

A terrible thought occurred to me.

"Do you think the aliens from the crashed ship got

them?" I asked. "Because I think I might have seen one in the tunnel a while back."

"You saw what?" he asked.

I told him about the green eyes I'd seen when I was on dust duty.

He turned pale and looked around. "I mean, if the aliens ate them, wouldn't there be blood?"

"Maybe they abducted them?"

Trey swallowed. "Let's get out of here," he said, and started walking.

"Are we going home?" I asked, catching up with him.

"No." He looked back at me. "We're going to the next settlement."

·ö·

As the train rumbled through the dark tunnel, I couldn't stop thinking about the former inhabitants. What had happened to them? Where had they gone?

"Do you think they got the virus, too?" I asked Trey.

"I don't know," he said. "Maybe."

"Which settlement is the next closest?" I asked.

"Russia or France, I think," he said, sounding frustrated. "I should have paid attention when Eliana lectured us."

"Me too," I said.

The light in the train flickered.

"What—" Trey started to say.

Then everything went dark. The train slowed until, finally, it stopped.

"What happened?" I asked Trey.

"I don't know!" I couldn't see him, but he sounded frantic. "I didn't do anything!"

We sat in the dark.

"What do we do?" I asked him.

"How do I know?"

I would've liked to hear some reassuring words right about now. Trey was no Albie—that was for sure.

"Do you have any glow sticks?" he asked me.

I handed one over, and a moment later, soft green light filled the dark train.

"Come here and hold it up so I can see the controls," Trey ordered.

I watched as Trey hit the power button again and again. But nothing happened.

"We've totally lost power," he said.

"Why?"

"Oh no," Trey said with a groan. "I think I know what's going on."

"What?"

"Eliana said she needed all the solar batteries she could get her hands on because of the storm. I think she took some off this train."

"And the one we have has run out of power?" I asked slowly.

His face was a sickly shade of green from the light. "Yeah."

Aw, dust it.

We were stuck.

Chapter Twenty

TRAPPED

I couldn't believe it. We were trapped in a vehicle.

Again.

At least I hadn't broken anything this time. But I did feel Vera's pain because I really needed to go to the bathroom. I should have gone in the Finnish settlement when I'd had a chance.

We discovered that Trey was right about the batteries: only one was connected, and it was drained. Once we realized we weren't going anywhere, we scrounged around the train for supplies. There were no emergency kits like in the rover. In fact, there was nothing.

"How long do you think we'll have to wait before someone finds us?" I asked Trey.

"We're not waiting. We're getting out of here!" He sounded so certain, almost like Albie. "We can walk to the next settlement. It's gotta be better than being stuck here in the dark."

It was hard to argue with that.

He slid open the train door. But the gap between the tunnel wall and the door was maybe six centimeters.

There was no way we could squeeze our bodies out.

"I don't believe this," Trey muttered.

"Let's just go out the back of the train," I said.

Except when we tried to open the door, it didn't budge.

"I think the latch is on the outside," Trey said. "Something about cargo falling out without it."

I thought of digi-reels I'd watched. People were always getting stuck in something called elevators. They would climb out through the roof.

"What about through the roof?" I suggested.

Most of the train was empty cargo space, but there were two low benches. Trey climbed on one and reached for the ceiling, but he was too short.

"Hold me up on your shoulders," I said.

But even with me sitting on Trey's shoulders, I couldn't reach the roof.

"There's always the front window?" I said. "We just need to break it and climb out that way."

"Worth a try," he said.

We searched for something that would break the window, only to find a plastic bucket. We took turns throwing it at the window, but it just bounced off. The window was too thick.

I looked at Trey. He'd gotten a lot bigger than me in the past two years. Meems said it was a growth spurt.

"Do you think you could kick the window in?" I asked Trey. "Like how Albie knocked open the door?"

He scowled at me. "Of course I can. Get out of the way."

I moved aside, then watched as he took a running leap at the window. He kicked out, like on one of the digi-reels with ninjas.

He yelped in pain. The window didn't budge.

Trey hopped around on one foot, holding the other.

"Are you okay?" I asked him.

"No! I am *not* okay!" he shouted. "That's the last time I listen to your dumb ideas!"

"It wasn't a dumb idea!"

"Yes, it was! You drive me nuts!"

"You drive me nuts, too!"

Trey slid to the floor, cradling his hurt foot. I sat across from him.

We sat in the dark, the green glow stick our only source of light.

"Do you think you broke it?" I asked him.

"No," he muttered.

"Sorry," I said.

His lips thinned. "It's okay."

We sat with the glow stick between us. It was so quiet down here. It made me wonder.

"You know the map?" I asked him.

He nodded.

"Why did we draw our Mars settlement aboveground?" I asked.

"What do you mean?"

I tried to explain. "It's dangerous to live up there because of the radiation and everything, right? So why did we plan our whole settlement on the surface?"

He looked thoughtful. "I think maybe because we wanted to be able to see things. Like in Earth cities. You can see vehicles and buildings. There's something nice about that."

"Yeah, that must be it," I agreed.

We stared at the glow stick.

"I have to go to the bathroom," I said.

"Me too," he said.

"What should we use?"

"The bucket, I guess."

So that's what we did.

Two hours later—or was it three?—we were *still* sitting in the train. I was exhausted, and I hadn't done anything. Worry makes you tired.

My brain wouldn't stop spinning. What had happened to the people from the Finnish settlement? Especially the kid with the cat-decorated room. Speaking of animals, where was the Earth chicken that laid the eggs in the kitchen? That made me think about the chocolate cake, and cake in general, especially carrot cake. Which reminded me of Phinneus and made me feel sad. And then I started wondering when someone at the settlement would realize what had happened to us.

As the light from the glow stick faded, my thoughts turned as dark as the inside of the train. And I got scared. Was this how Lissa felt as she waited in the rover? Had she been hopeful at first? Then as the hours ticked by, did she slowly realize that no one was coming? That they'd left her behind? Forgotten all about her?

I shivered. I missed my cozy quilt.

"What if no one finds us?" I asked suddenly.

Trey didn't say anything, and panic raced up my spine.

"No one even knows we're stuck here!" I said, and my chest felt tighter and tighter.

He looked at me.

"Don't you get it? No one's coming to help us! No one—"

Trey interrupted me. "Three-word story, Bell."

I was so startled, the words got stuck in my throat.

"What?" I finally choked out.

"I'll go first," he said, as if everything was just fine. "Once upon a . . ."

I shook my head.

"Come on, Bell, your turn," he insisted. "Once upon a . . ."

I blew out a breath. Fine. ". . . time, we were . . ."

". . . stuck in a . . . ," Trey said.

". . . train in a . . . ," I said.

". . . tunnel, and I . . . ," Trey said.

". . . was totally bored," I said.

"So I farted!" he said.

I burst out laughing. He still had it.

We still had it.

"Again?" I asked him.

He gave a weak smile. "Only if I get to go first."

·☼·

We played round after round after round of three-word story. It almost made me forget we were stuck in the train.

Then the glow stick winked out, and we were in the dark.

"I'll open another one," I said, digging in my pocket.

"Don't!" Trey said. "There's only two glow sticks left. We should keep them for emergencies."

"So we just sit here in the dark?"

"Why don't we take a nap?" Trey suggested. "It'll help pass the time."

I lay down on one of the benches, and Trey took the other. It was like we were back to sharing a room. Except in a cold, dark tunnel.

"Why did you move rooms?" I asked Trey. "What did I do?"

Trey sighed. "You didn't do anything. I just wanted Sai to take me on as his apprentice."

I was so confused. "But what does that have to do with switching rooms?"

"You're the youngest, and I thought maybe you were holding me back, I guess. That Sai saw me as young, like you. I thought if I changed rooms, he'd realize I am older."

I couldn't see his face, but I heard it in his voice. He sounded almost apologetic.

"Anyway," he said with a bitter laugh, "being in charge isn't all it's cracked up to be, huh?"

We lay there in the dark.

"You know what?" I said. "If I had to be stuck in this train, I'm glad I'm stuck with you."

"Really?"

"Yeah. Have you heard Albie snore?"

We both laughed.

Finally, I drifted off to sleep.

I dreamt I was back home and everything was fine. I was in the algae farm with Phinneus. He was wearing his blue sweater.

"Phinneus!" I said. "I missed you so much!"

"I've been here the whole time," Phinneus said, his eyes crinkling.

"But you haven't," I told him. "You—you—were—"

I couldn't bring myself to say the word.

"I want to show you what I've been growing," he said, and pointed to a pot of Earth soil.

A tall bright-yellow flower with a big brown center was growing in it.

"It's a sunflower," he said. "I grew them in my garden in New California."

"It's so big," I said.

"You'll be taller than it soon. You've grown so much," he said.

Something cold whipped through the algae farm.

"Here," Phinneus said, taking off his sweater and handing it to me. "I think you'll need this."

"Why?"

"It'll keep you warm," he said. "The wind's picking up."

"The wind?"

He tilted his head. "Can't you feel it? Wake up, Bell."

I blinked my eyes open. Everything was dark. I thought maybe I was back home, but then I remembered the train. The lack of snoring gave it away. Also, it was freezing cold. I shivered as icy air blew against my cheek.

Wind?

It was coming from somewhere near my head.

I pulled one of the glow sticks from my pocket, snapped it on, and scrambled down to the floor. There was a latch on the side of the bench. I pulled it and discovered the source of the cold air: a small panel opened onto the track.

"Trey!" I shouted. "Trey!"

He opened his eyes and sat up abruptly, looking confused. "What—what are you doing? I thought I told you not to use the glow stick!"

"I found a way out!"

Trey scrambled to his feet. "What? Where?"

"Right here! Under the bench!"

He knelt and peered through the open panel. His face filled with excitement.

"Move," he told me, and pushed me out of his way. Then he stuck his head through it and started to wedge his way in. But he didn't get far.

"Ugh!" he shouted, and pulled back out with a huff. "I can't fit through the space! I'm too big!"

I looked at him.

"But I'm not," I said.

Chapter Twenty-One

DARKNESS

In digi-reels, before one person has to go on a dangerous mission, there's usually a tearful scene. Another person tells them to be careful and never give up hope.

Instead of a touching farewell, Trey and I had a fight over glow sticks.

"Take them both!" he insisted. "I'll be fine."

But I knew him better. After all, I had shared a room with him for most of my life. We'd always had a night-light because neither of us liked total darkness.

"I just need one," I said, handing the unlit glow stick back to him. "You can have the other."

"Fine," he huffed.

Then I crouched down by the hatch, hesitating. I couldn't seem to make my body move. I was scared.

"I would go instead of you if I could," Trey said.

"I know," I said, and took a deep breath. "All right, here goes."

I tossed the lit glow stick onto the track and carefully squeezed through the hatch onto the ground. A moment later, the unused glow stick plopped down next to me.

"Hey!" I shouted, waving it. "Take it back."

"No way," Trey said. "You need it more than me."

"But you'll be sitting in the dark!" I said.

"And you'll be walking in the dark." He barked a laugh. "It's not like I'm going anywhere."

I clutched the glow sticks, fear dancing up my back. "I don't know if I can do this," I confessed.

"Just pretend the tunnel is the corridor outside our bedroom, and it won't be scary," Trey said. "Be brave, Bell-Bell!"

And just like that, something was right again. Even though our world was falling apart, Trey was still my best friend. He would literally sit in the dark for me.

But instead of his doing everything for me, like when I was little, it was my turn to do something for him. I had to be our voice now and get help.

I crawled out until I was standing in front of the train, the endless black tunnel before me. I turned and waved at Trey. I couldn't see him. But I knew he waved back.

Then I started walking.

The first glow stick didn't last long. It had been fading when I'd set off. So I clicked open the last one and continued on.

But being somewhere so dark was completely unnerving. To stop focusing on the darkness, I made up a little game. I began reciting all the animal names I remembered from my book.

Koala.

Whale.

Moray eel.

Panda.

Snake.

Something unseen slithered against my foot. I yelped. A snake? When I looked down, all I saw was the track. I started walking again.

Hedgehog.

Flamingo.

Bat.

I heard a rustle of wings. Didn't bats hang on ceilings? I held the glow stick up and squinted at the ceiling, but I didn't see anything. I shook my head. Maybe I was just hungry? I hadn't eaten since breakfast, and that was a long time ago.

Hummingbird.

Orangutan.

Squirrel.

Crocodile.

Teeth. Big teeth . . . that like to eat children and . . .

Maybe this wasn't such a fun game after all.

My imagination was way too realistic.

·ö·

It turned out all those horror digi-reels got it wrong. The scariest thing in the world wasn't a monster or an alien chasing you. It wasn't killer slime mold or zombie plague.

It was being alone.

My whole life, I'd had people around me. The settlement was small and crowded, and someone was always in your space. Meems joked that she couldn't burp without someone hearing her. But I would have given just about anything to hear a burp now. I even missed the sound of Albie snoring. Honestly, I would have been happy to talk to an alien. At least then I wouldn't be alone. Maybe it would even play three-word story with me.

I had to force my legs to keep moving. Take a few steps. Hold out the glow stick. Make sure there was nothing in the shadows ahead. Take a few more steps. Repeat. It was like a digi-reel playing the same scene over and over. How had I ever thought this was a good idea? Why hadn't I just waited with Trey to be rescued? What was I—

I tripped over my own foot and fell.

My knee hit the ground hard, and something in me

snapped. Before I could think it through, I was up and rushing the other way, to the train. Back to Trey and safety. This was too much. Like Albie had said.

I was just a kid, and I wasn't brave.

So I ran as fast as I could down the dark tunnel, my heart pounding and pain shooting up my knee. I don't know how far I'd gotten when an image of Meems's face flashed in front of my eyes, and I stumbled. I pictured Sai's beard and heard Darby's belly laugh, and my feet slowed. I smelled Salty Bill's cooking and finally stopped.

They were my family.

And I would lose them—just like I'd lost Phinneus—if I didn't get help.

So I took a deep breath. Then I turned around and started walking toward the next settlement.

My knee was throbbing now and my glow stick had started to fade. I didn't know how much farther I had to walk. The tunnel stretched for kilometers around all the settlements. In places, it curved because of some obstacle. As the tunnel slowly grew darker, everything seemed louder: my footsteps, my breathing, even my rumbling stomach. But there was also a sound I couldn't quite identify: a brief, high-pitched cry that echoed down the tunnel.

It sounded eerily like a small child crying.

Was someone else in the tunnel? Maybe one of those kids from the Finnish settlement? Were they hurt?

"Hello?" I called. "Is someone there?"

I heard the cry again, and it sounded closer.

"Are you okay?" I asked. "My name's Bell, and I'm from the American settlement."

As I walked around a curve, I saw the eyes in the darkness. But they didn't belong to a child.

Because children didn't have glowing green eyes.

They were the same alien eyes I'd seen on dust duty!

I gasped and the alien disappeared in the darkness. In the next heartbeat, it reappeared, closer. What did you say to an alien?

"Uh, hi, nice alien," I babbled. "Don't eat me. I'm not very tasty and, uh, I'm probably pretty smelly, too, since I haven't had a hot shower in a while."

The alien didn't seem to care, because it kept coming.

I squeezed my eyes shut, too terrified to move.

"Meow."

Chapter Twenty-Two

FOLLOW

Leo stood in the tunnel like it was something he did every day.

"Leo!" I cried, grabbing him.

How did he get here? Had he followed me? Then I decided I didn't care because I had my little buddy! I hugged Leo tight. He purred, his tail flapping lazily. For a brief moment, everything seemed better in the world because I wasn't alone anymore.

"I'm so glad to see you," I told him.

He rubbed his nose against my chin, marking me as his. I was part of his pride. Or maybe he was part of mine.

"What are you doing here?" I asked him.

He squirmed out of my grasp and leapt gracefully to the ground.

"Meeee-ow!" Leo said. *I'm hungry!*

"Me too," I said. "But I don't have any um-yums for you."

He stalked down the tunnel.

"Hey! Wait for me!" I called.

I didn't have much choice but to follow my cat. At least he seemed to know where he was going. Once in a while, Leo looked back at me, and I saw his green eyes flash in the dark. And I'd thought he was an alien! How did he get into the tunnel? Was he chasing some of the mice that had gotten away?

We walked for a while, and as we approached a curve, I saw a trickle of light spilling out. Then I saw it: a red-white-and-blue flag hanging next to a door with a light.

I'd made it to the French settlement!

Leo leapt up on the landing and started meowing at the door.

I didn't know what to do. Was it more dangerous to keep walking? Would the French attack me with their stick weapons if they saw me?

Leo pawed at the door, meowing to be let in.

Could I trust my cat? Surely he wouldn't lead me into a dangerous situation, right? After all, I'd been following him around my whole life.

"Mwar!" Leo said insistently. *Let me in!*

"Okay," I told him. "I sure hope you're right."

I opened the door and followed Leo inside.

Unlike at the Finnish settlement, there were clear signs of life everywhere—from bright daytime lighting to toasty-warm air. And there was music. Old-fashioned Earth music, the kind with violins. If Albie was here, he would know what it was called. As we got closer to the source of the music, I heard laughing and clapping. Someone shouted, *"Bisou bisou!"*

What did that mean? What was a *bisou?*

Leo stopped in front of a door and meowed. I pushed it open and looked around in wonder. Or maybe shock. Festive decorations hung everywhere. The room was full of grown-ups and kids wearing colored-paper hats. A woman and a man were dancing in the middle of the floor. The woman wore a long, fluttery white dress Flossy would have loved. The man spun and dipped the woman, and everyone clapped.

Off to the side was a table piled high with all sorts of food. In the center was the tallest cake I'd ever seen. It was three levels high, and on top were two tiny dolls.

I had walked right into the middle of a . . . *party?*

Across the room, my eyes met those of a little girl clutching a teddy bear. She tugged on the arm of the man next to her and pointed at me. His mouth dropped open. One by one, people stopped talking to stare at me. Finally, everyone—even the couple, who had stopped dancing—was staring as I stood there nervously, the music playing on.

A woman stepped forward. Her gray hair was cut in a sharp bob. I couldn't look away from the ragged white scar on her forehead: that had to have hurt.

"*D'où viens-tu, mon cher?*" she said, tilting her head questioningly.

"Um, *bonjour?*" I said.

She gave me an odd look. "*Es-tu blessé?*"

But my brain short-circuited, and I couldn't remember any other French words.

"*Bonjour.*"

"*As-tu des problèmes?*" she asked, her gaze serious.

"*Bonjour.*"

She shook her head as if mystified. Then, to my complete shock, she asked, "Are you American?"

I nodded.

"What is your name?"

"Bell."

"One last question," she said.

I swallowed. This was it. It was going to be bad.

"Do you like cake?"

I smiled.

The woman told me her name was Commander Sylvie Laurent. She sat me at a table and handed me a slice of cake and a glass of water. Then she sat down across from me.

"Now tell me what happened, Bell," she said in a gentle voice.

It all spilled out of me in a rush. The mice. Phinneus dying. The storm. The grown-ups being sick. Running out of medicine. The response from Earth. Everything falling apart. Us going for help. Trey stuck in the train. Following Leo.

"What about Commander Sai?" she asked, looking at me steadily.

"He's sick, too," I said.

Her expression didn't change. "I see."

I took a bite of the cake. It was chocolate and delicious. Probably the most delicious cake I'd ever eaten.

"How long have you children been managing things on your own?" she asked.

"Um, a few weeks, I think? You know, this is really good cake!"

Her eyes closed briefly.

"You don't have to worry anymore, *mon cher*," she said, and it sounded like a promise. "We'll take care of everything."

I watched in a daze as she calmly gave orders,

organizing a party to take medicine to our settlement and another group to rescue Trey.

A girl with two braids walked over, carrying Leo.

"Is this your cat?" she asked.

But all I could do was stare at her hair. It was *red*!

"Is it real?" I whispered.

She scrunched her eyes. "Is what real?"

"Your hair," I said.

"Of course it's real!" she huffed.

I shook my head in amazement. Flossy was right.

"So is this your cat?" she asked me.

"Yes, this is Leo," I said.

"Do you feed him?" she asked.

"Of course," I said. "Why?"

"He's been coming here for months, and we give him food," she explained. "We were wondering who he belonged to and why they were not feeding him."

"He just likes to eat," I explained.

"I'm Amélie," she said. "What's your name?"

"Bell," I said.

"Are you really an American? I've never seen one," she admitted.

"Yes," I said. "What are you?"

"French, of course," she said, like I should know. She reminded me of Vera.

A boy with straight black hair joined us. He couldn't take his eyes off Leo. "That's your cat, then?"

"I told you, Wei," Amélie said in an important voice. "The cat belongs to the Americans."

"You don't have any cats?" I asked him.

"The Chinese have chickens," Amélie said, like it was perfectly obvious.

I remembered the eggs.

"You know," Wei said, "you don't look like what I imagined an American would look like."

"Really?"

He nodded. "They say the Americans always wear their uniforms."

"Just Sai," I said. "He's our commander."

"This party is boring!" Amélie complained.

"It's true," Wei agreed. Then he smiled at me. "You're the most exciting thing that's happened!"

"All they've been doing is *bisou bisou*," Amélie said.

"What's *bisou bisou*?" I asked.

"Kiss kiss," she said, making a kissing face. "Blech!"

"What is the party for?" I asked.

"It's a wedding," Amélie said. "Brigitte, who's from our settlement, is marrying Oskar, who's Finnish."

"The Finnish settlement? Does that mean they haven't been eaten or abducted by the aliens?" I asked.

Amélie gave me a funny look. "Aliens? Are Americans crazy?"

"You don't understand! We were just at the Finnish settlement, and no one was there!" I told her.

"That's because they're all here for the wedding," Wei explained.

"Oh," I said.

"Do you like Ping-Pong?" Amélie asked me.

"What's Ping-Pong?"

"You don't know what Ping-Pong is?" Wei asked.

I shook my head.

"Come on," Amélie said in a bossy voice. "We'll show you."

Everywhere I looked, there was something to see. Colorful posters. Tiny blinking lights that hung from the ceiling. They even had real musical instruments. Albie was going to explode when he saw them.

"Is that a violin?" I asked.

Amélie nodded. "Do you play?"

I shook my head.

"Then you're lucky!" she said. "I am forced to practice three days a week. It is the bane of my existence!"

Amélie opened a door, and I followed her and Wei into a room where a bunch of kids were standing around. In the middle of the room was a large rectangular table, and it had a net, like the one at the Finnish settlement. A boy and a girl were hitting a small white ball back and forth with the plate things. The ball bounced over the net.

"That's Ping-Pong," Wei said.

I guess the table in the Finnish settlement wasn't for eating.

"*Everyone!*" Amélie called. "This is Bell! He is a real, live American. He is the owner of the cat."

The blond boy at the table gasped. "That's your cat? You should feed him!"

"We do feed him," I said. "He's just always hungry."

"That's Taavi," Amélie told me. "He's from the Finnish settlement. He loves cats."

I was pretty sure I had been in this kid's room.

"Do you want to play?" the cat-loving boy asked me.

"I don't know how," I admitted.

"It's easy," he said. "I'll teach you."

It wasn't hard to learn, and it was a lot of fun. We played game after game, switching partners, sometimes even playing with teams of two. Amélie introduced me to all the other kids, and I was surprised to learn that they were all from different countries—France, Russia, China, Finland.

"Do you do this a lot?" I asked.

"Play Ping-Pong?" Wei asked.

I struggled to explain. "I meant get together with the other countries."

"Of course!" Amélie said. "I would go bonkers if I was here all the time. Do you have any idea how boring that would be? Also, I would have to practice the violin! Can you imagine anything worse?"

"Besides," Taavi said, "the Russian settlement has the best chocolate candies on Mars. There's nothing more important than candy."

It was hard to argue with that.

Chapter Twenty-Three

VACATION

By that evening, Albie, Flossy, Vera, and Trey had joined me in the French settlement. Like me, they all seemed a little stunned to find themselves there.

"Volunteers from the various countries will stay in your settlement to nurse the sick and manage the chores," Commander Laurent told us. "You children have handled enough already, so you'll remain here until everyone is healthy again."

The French fed us a big meal, then set us up in comfortable bedrooms. We even got to take hot showers, since they had a different energy technology than we did and weren't affected by the storm as much.

But despite being clean and fed and warm, we were uneasy. We'd never slept anywhere but our own home. Now we were in this foreign place with people we didn't know.

Vera seemed especially suspicious.

"Why are they being so nice to us?" she asked as we

all huddled in the bedroom I was sharing with Trey and Albie.

Albie shrugged. "Maybe they are actually nice?"

"You didn't see them chasing us with those weapons!" Vera told him.

"They did rescue me from the train," Trey said.

"But what if we're wrong about them?" Vera asked. "What if they're *not* good people?"

Flossy, who had been uncharacteristically quiet, said, "Vera's got a point. Remember what Sai told us, about how they left Lissa to die? I don't know if we can trust them."

No one said anything for a moment.

"They've been feeding Leo for months," I told them.

"Now we know why he's been getting so fat," Albie said with a wry look.

"I think anyone who takes care of a cat is probably good," I said.

But Vera wasn't convinced.

"We'll see," she said.

Amélie showed me around the settlement. Things were different there. For one, it was much bigger, with more people. There was even a baby human. I had never seen one in real life, just in digi-reels.

We watched as the baby shoveled algae porridge into his mouth with a spoon. Most of it ended up on his shirt or his face or the floor.

"What's the baby's name?" I asked.

"Theo," his mother told me. She had algae porridge all over her shirt, courtesy of her child.

Amélie turned to me. "They should've named him Poopoo. His diapers smell terrible."

As we walked down the corridors, we passed people from different countries coming and going. It was still hard to absorb that the other countries were in daily contact. They traded all sorts of goods, too. Which is how I got to try my first Earth chicken egg.

The French cook "scrambled" it for me and served it with toast for breakfast. The egg looked fluffy, like yellow clouds.

"Well?" Amélie asked. "Do you like it?"

"It's delicious," I said.

When I'd cleaned my plate, I asked the cook if I could have more.

"Of course," he told me.

"Why does everyone speak English?" I asked him.

"It's the common language for space," he said. "If a Russian ship and a Chinese ship need to communicate, they'll use English. That's why we all know it."

After breakfast, Amélie and I went upstairs to the

communications room. We were both curious about the storm.

"*Bonjour*, Armand," Amélie said to a gray-haired man sitting behind a desk.

"*Bonjour*, Amélie," he said with a smile. But when he saw me, he turned pale, like he'd seen a ghost.

"You!" he exclaimed. "You were the child I saw in the rover!"

I stepped back nervously. "You were the one who chased us with those weapons?"

"What weapons?" Amélie asked.

"They were waving metal weapons at us! Like Earth swords!"

Armand burst out laughing. "Those were golf clubs!"

"What?"

Amélie rolled her eyes. Honestly, she could seriously give Vera a run for her money when it came to attitude.

"You hit a ball with them," she said. "It's a game."

Armand walked over to a corner and pulled out one of the golf clubs. Then he put a ball on the floor and gently hit it.

"That's what we were doing," he said.

Amélie seemed unimpressed. "Ping-Pong is much more fun."

"Why did you chase us?" I asked him.

"Children should not be driving rovers," Armand said

dryly. "In fact, I tried contacting the American settlement using the old line, but we were blocked and couldn't get a message through. I can't imagine Commander Sai was happy to learn that you had taken a rover."

"You know Sai?" I asked.

"Of course," Armand said, pointing to a digi-pic taped to the wall. It was a picture of a party. There was a younger Sai, dressed like an Earth pirate. Next to him was a young version of Commander Laurent. She was in a similar getup. There were other familiar faces as well: Darby and Eliana, Salty Bill, and Phinneus. They were all wearing costumes.

"That was a very famous Halloween party," he told me. "Your Commander Sai and our Commander Laurent won for best costume," he told me. "They were a pair of pirates."

I remembered the award in Sai's box.

Amélie grabbed my arm. "Come on," she said. "I have a lot more to show you!"

As we walked away, Armand called to me, "Welcome to the French settlement, Bell. Don't drive any rovers."

⚙

As the days passed, we became more comfortable. Everyone was so kind and tried to put us at ease. Also, our grown-ups were slowly getting better. The Finnish doctor was staying at our settlement and expected them to make a full recovery. Finally, the knot of worry that we had been carrying loosened.

I remembered Meems telling me about an Earth practice called taking a vacation. People would go somewhere and do nothing except maybe eat or lie on the beach. Being in the French settlement felt like taking a vacation. While there was no beach, it was relaxing, and we did a lot of eating. My favorite dish was something called a *crêpe*, a thin pancake with chocolate sauce. It was the most perfect meal ever invented: breakfast and dessert rolled into one.

The best part was simply being around other kids my age. Taavi and Wei visited every few days. Along with Amélie, we spent hours together playing Ping-Pong. Taavi said I was a natural. Maybe my gift was being good at playing Ping-Pong?

Trey and another boy, Rémy, spent their time riding on a board with wheels—a "skateboard"—up and down the long corridors. To be fair, Trey spent a lot of that time falling off the skateboard, but he seemed pretty happy to be doing it.

Flossy, naturally, was obsessed with how the French dressed. She and her new friends spent hours creating outfits and debating fashion.

Then there was Albie. Sweet, kind Albie couldn't seem to remember how to speak when he was anywhere near a French girl named Layla. She had long dark hair and a warm smile. I didn't understand what it was about her that made Albie start stammering. It was as if his mouth forgot how to work.

Amélie and I were watching a digi-reel with Layla in the recreation room when Albie walked in. He saw us and froze.

"*Bonjour*, Albie," Layla said.

"Uh, uh, uh," he said. "Hi."

"Would you like to join us?" she asked him. "We're watching a digi-reel of a music concert on Earth."

A look of pure terror crossed his face.

"Uh, no thanks!" he shouted, and practically ran out of the room.

Layla turned to me, a quizzical look on her face. "Does he not like music?"

"He loves music," I told her.

"Oh," she said.

"Albie can be a little shy, I guess."

"He seems very nice," she mused.

"He is," I assured her. "Except for the snoring part."

But despite all the kindness, Vera remained suspicious. Of the food. Of the people. Even the shampoo.

"Is my hair supposed to be this shiny?" she asked me.

Her hair looked soft and lovely. I didn't understand what she was so upset about.

"At least it's clean," I told her. "Can you pass me another madeleine?"

She and I were having an afternoon snack in the kitchen. The cook had made something called madeleines, which were mini-cakes in the shape of an Earth shell. They were delicious.

A man with dark curly hair and thick glasses walked over to our table.

"*Bonjour*," he said.

"*Bonjour*," I said, but Vera didn't say anything.

"I'm Gaspard," he said. "Do you remember me, Vera?"

I was expecting her to say something snarky, but instead she just stared at him.

Then the man started singing in French. It sounded like a lullaby.

Au clair de la lune
Mon ami Pierrot
Prête-moi ta plume
Pour écrire un mot

Vera's eyes widened and her lips trembled. "Are you—are you my *nanny*?"

"Oui," he said, and smiled. "It's very good to see you, Vera."

Vera leapt up, threw her arms around him, and started crying.

He patted her back and smiled fondly. "It's nice to see you haven't changed."

My favorite place here, too, was the algae farm. Like us, the French grew lots of algae, plus vegetables and fruit—tomatoes, green beans, strawberries, and lettuces. But they also grew Earth flowers in all sorts of colors.

The person in charge of the farm was named Jules, and she took great delight in showing me her experiments. Right now, she was growing something called a lemon tree. It didn't look like much at the moment, but she said it would eventually smell delicious.

Just being in the farm was comforting. It reminded me of Phinneus. I could hear his voice in the hum of the soft lights. See him in the green shoots of the hydroponic pots. I knew he would love it here. He would be curious, taking notes and asking questions.

Tell me, he would say, *what kind of fertilizer? Which seeds? How much light?*

One afternoon, I was wandering around the farm

when I spotted Commander Laurent. She was cutting some purple flowers.

She saw me and smiled. "*Bonjour*, Bell."

"What are you doing?" I asked her.

"Well," she said, sitting back on her heels, "this is called lavender. I'll dry it, put it in fabric pouches, and stick them under my pillow. The scent of lavender is very good for sleep."

"Huh," I said. "Does it help with snoring?"

She laughed and shook her head. "I'm afraid not."

"Too bad," I said.

"Tell me," she said. "How are you finding things here?"

"Good," I said. "I really like the food. And Ping-Pong!"

"I'm glad to hear that," she said.

"Why do you grow flowers?" I asked.

Her eyes crinkled. "What do you mean?"

"Do you eat them or use them for medicine?"

She shook her head, looking amused. "We grow them because they're beautiful. Everyone needs joy."

I guess that was as good a reason as any.

"I was very sorry to hear about Phinneus's passing," she told me.

My head shot up. "You knew him?"

"*Oui*," she said. "We worked together on adapting the algae-growing process for Mars. He was a brilliant and gentle man, and I learned a lot from him."

"I miss him," I admitted.

"Of course you do," she said. "He was a wonderful person. It's terribly hard to lose someone you love."

"How do I stop missing him?" I asked her.

"By remembering him," she said simply.

I shook my head.

"Tell me your favorite memories of Phinneus," she urged.

"He was a farmer on Earth. In a place called New California. Bunnies lived in his yard," I said.

"Go on," she encouraged me.

"His wife made good carrot cake. When I was little, he would carry me around the farm on his shoulders. He taught me how to plant seeds, and he kept cookies in a jar on his desk just for me."

"If you remember all these things, he'll never really be gone," she told me.

I didn't say anything.

"Now, would you like to help me plant some herbs?"

"Sure," I said.

As we walked to get supplies, I asked her, "Have you heard about the evil Earth plants called weeds?"

⚛

The teenagers got together and decided to throw a party. Mostly because they wanted to dance.

"We want to try old Earth styles!" Flossy said.

They invited kids from all the settlements and pushed the furniture against the walls of the recreation room. Music blared as the teens did all sorts of dances.

They started doing the Charleston, swinging their arms and moving their legs back and forth. Then they did the moonwalk, gliding backward while they looked like they were stepping forward. (I didn't understand what the moon had to do with it.) Finally, they tried vogueing, which was just posing with their hands in weird positions.

Trey came over to me with Rémy. "Bell! Bell! You'll never believe this!"

"What?" I asked.

"I found out what happened to the digi-cam outside," Trey said. "The one that was broken."

Rémy gave a sheepish look. "Uh, yeah, sorry about that."

"It was you? How?"

"A couple of us sort of borrowed a rover and drove to your settlement. I guess we weren't paying attention, and we hit the pole. It was an accident," he said with a wince.

I shook my head.

"What were you doing by our settlement?" I asked.

"We were just curious," Rémy said with a shrug.

It was oddly reassuring to know we weren't the only kids on Mars who got into trouble.

After watching the teens do an Earth dance called break

dancing, which involved spinning on the floor, Amélie turned to me.

"I'm hungry," she said. "Let's get some of those cookies before they eat them all!"

We were walking back from the kitchen, our pockets stuffed with cookies, when Amélie elbowed me. She pointed down the hall. There, in a darkened alcove, were Albie and Layla.

And they were kissing!

"Bisou bisou!" Amélie said, and made a kissy face.

"Blech," I said, and she nodded.

It didn't matter where we were from. We could all agree that teenagers were strange.

Chapter Twenty-Four

HOME AGAIN

After almost a month, our vacation at the French settlement was coming to an end.

Commander Laurent said it was finally safe for us to return home. But I was a little conflicted.

Part of me was excited. I missed so many things. My own bed. Meems's laughter. Salty Bill's cooking. I even missed Sai's emergency drills. Most of all, I was eager to see with my own eyes that they were all healthy and well. I wanted to erase the last image of them I had in my mind: lying sick in bed and coughing.

But another part of me was sad to leave the new things I had discovered at the French settlement. Tasty *crêpes*. Ping-Pong. Stinky babies. Most of all, my new friends, Wei and Taavi and Amélie. Would I be able to see them again?

"Do you think we'll get to come back?" I asked.

It was late, and we were all in bed. The room was quiet for the moment because Albie was still awake.

"I don't know," Trey said. "I hope so."

Albie was more confident. "I'm sure Sai will be okay with it. After all, look at what they've done for us!"

I felt a little better.

And then Albie started snoring.

"Psst! Bell!" Trey whispered. "You awake?"

"Yep," I said. "Who can sleep with Albie's snoring?"

"Maybe when we get home, we can switch rooms again?"

"Socksy!" I said.

He laughed. "Now I know why Vera and Flossy were so happy to have me in their room."

On the morning of our departure, all the kids came to see us off. There were presents and lots of tears, mostly from the teenagers.

My friends brought me treats. Wei gave me a bag of eggs, which Salty Bill would love. Taavi gave me a small plastic cat.

"It looks just like Leo!" I said.

"It is him!" He beamed. "I made it myself!"

Amélie handed me a bag with dramatic flair.

"My present is the best!" she announced.

"It's a Ping-Pong paddle!" I exclaimed. Then my face fell. "But I don't have a Ping-Pong table."

"Exactly," Amélie said with a sly wink. "This way, you'll have to come back here to play with us."

I almost started crying.

But before I could, Commander Laurent walked up to me with a shy look and handed me a bouquet of daisies.

"Thanks!" I told her.

She leaned down and whispered in my ear, "Actually, they're for Commander Sai."

"Commander Sai?"

"He'll understand what they mean," she told me. "It's an old Earth custom."

"I'll give them to him," I promised her.

Then it was time to board the train home. Albie was the last to get on. As we pulled away from the dock, I looked back and saw Layla.

She was wearing Albie's ball cap.

⚛

Armand drove us back to our settlement on the French train.

Sai was waiting on the dark platform with a glow stick when we arrived. His face was thinner, but he seemed rested—like he'd finally had a good night's sleep. I'd never realized how tired he always looked. Which made sense, I guessed. After all, he was in charge. It wasn't like he could take a vacation.

"Here they are, Sai. Safe and sound," Armand said with a smile.

"Thank you," Sai told him.

Then we were rushing through the door and down the corridor. I smelled a scent that's impossible to describe.

It smelled like home.

"They're here!" someone shouted—maybe Salty Bill?—and we were surrounded by hugs.

"Meems!" I cried, hugging her tight.

"Oh, Bell," she said. "I think you've grown!"

I thought of everything I'd experienced in the French settlement. Maybe I *had* grown a little.

My eyes carefully cataloged them one by one. Meems's eyes were bright, and her cheeks were rosy. Salty Bill had shaved his beard, and he looked years younger. Eliana and Darby were their old selves.

"Where did you get those flowers?" Meems asked.

"Oh," I said. "Commander Laurent gave them to me to give to Sai."

Meems raised an eyebrow. "Really?"

"Here you go," I told Sai, handing him the flowers.

His hands shook a little as he took them. "Well," he muttered, and looked down fast.

That evening, Salty Bill made a big welcome-home dinner with all our favorite foods. I looked around the table at everyone's smiling faces.

"We're very glad you children are home," Darby said. "This place hasn't been the same without you."

"Did you know they have a baby in the French settlement?" Flossy said. "He's so cute!"

"Except when he cries," I said.

"I met my nanny," Vera said. "Gaspard said I was a very good baby."

"And there was a big dance party, and everyone came!" Flossy explained. "We danced all night and stayed up until morning and then had breakfast!"

The grown-ups looked at each other.

"Who's 'everyone'?" Sai asked.

"All the kids from the other settlements," Flossy said, and ticked them off on her fingers. "Mischa, Tatiana, Lok, Layla, Kerttu . . ."

"I see," Sai said, and frowned.

"Why did you all lie to us?" Vera asked in her usual blunt way.

Sai raised an eyebrow. "Lie?"

"About the other countries being dangerous! They're not dangerous! They're fun."

Sai stood up stiffly. "Excuse me. I need to go check on the weather."

After he'd left the room, Vera shook her head. "Really,"

she muttered. "If we lied half as much as grown-ups do, we'd be in time-out forever."

⬥

Our home looked better than it ever had, and not just because I'd missed it. The rescue team had been busy. In addition to nursing our grown-ups back to health, they'd repaired things. Everywhere I looked, there were improvements.

They'd fixed the light timer. They'd installed a new kind of battery charger so we didn't have to ration power and could have hot showers. Salty Bill's cabinets were full of interesting ingredients they'd donated—different spices and flours and bars of chocolate. They'd even planted new vegetables and fruits in the algae farm.

The biggest difference was in Sai's workshop. His shelves were practically overflowing with supplies—most of which I'd never seen before.

"What's this?" I asked Sai, picking up a rubber blob-shaped thing. It was tacky and squishy at the same time.

"A kind of bonding agent," he said, his fingers hovering over his digi-slate. "It works better than duct tape, supposedly."

The flowers from Commander Laurent were in a plastic jar of water on his desk.

"What does it mean?" I asked him.

"What does what mean?"

"Commander Laurent said giving someone flowers was an Earth tradition," I said. "What does it mean?"

Sai's face turned beet red. "Yes, well, it has many different meanings, I suppose. Friendship, of course."

I remembered the digi-pic of him and Commander Laurent dressed as pirates. "You were friends with Commander Laurent?"

"Yes," he said, looking down.

"Did you play Ping-Pong with her?"

"Ping-Pong?"

"We played it every day at the French settlement. Commander Laurent played against me a few times," I said. "She's really good at it!"

He barked a laugh. "I remember. She's the most brilliant woman I've ever met," he said, and he looked sad.

I changed the subject. "What are you working on?" I asked him.

He rubbed his forehead. "Writing a situation report to send to Command. I need to fill them in on everything that's happened since we were rescued."

"Can you ask them to send kittens?"

I was just joking.

"After everything you children have been through, you certainly deserve a kitten," he said, a solemn look on his face.

I didn't know what to say.

"Bell," Sai said, "Trey told me what happened on the train. It was very, very brave of you to walk through the tunnel by yourself to get help."

But he was wrong. I hadn't been brave.

"I almost gave up. I was scared the whole time," I confessed.

His eyes met mine, and he nodded.

"That's what bravery feels like," he said.

I was happy to be back in my own bed. There was no denying the comfort of being home. And I was looking forward to some changes. Trey was moving back in with me, and Albie would be moving into Phinneus's old room.

As much as I loved Albie, I was getting a little sick of the sad music. Albie kept playing the same three songs over and over and over again. He was doing it now, lying in bed and staring at the ceiling as the music played. The songs were about broken hearts, lost love, and being alone forever. They were worse than the snoring.

"Albie," I finally said, "can you maybe play something else? It doesn't have to be happy, just not so sad."

He sighed and clicked off the music. He whispered, "I miss her so much, Bell."

It wasn't hard to figure out who he was talking about. Layla.

"Every single second of the day, I wonder what she's doing," he said. "What is she thinking? What is she eating?"

"You think about what she's eating? Really?"

"I'm in love, Bell," he said.

I wasn't sure what else to say. This seemed like a conversation he should be having with Flossy. She had a lot of opinions on romance. Well, mostly what to wear when falling in love.

"What am I going to do next?" he asked me.

"Well, supper's in half an hour," I said.

"Not now," he said. "I mean in the future. I want to see her again. I can't just *forget*."

I understood what Albie meant. I couldn't stop thinking about everything I'd seen and experienced in the other settlements. It was like having a bite of delicious cake: I wanted more.

"Maybe you can ask Sai if we can have a visit?" I suggested.

"I did," Albie confessed. "He said no."

I wasn't surprised. "Did he give a reason?"

"Sai said the illness was a crisis situation. But things are back to normal now. It's not fair."

That's when I knew how upset Albie was, because he

never disagreed with Sai. It was like watching a small crack start to form.

Albie clicked the music back on and rolled over to face the wall, making a noise that sounded suspiciously like a sob.

The sad song swelled in our room.

DATE: 10.1.2091
FROM: CDR Dexter
TO: US Terrestrial Command
MESSAGE: Situation Report

After it was determined that our crew would not survive without the viral medication, it was decided that some of our members would seek aid from the French settlement. They had a supply of medication on hand and donated it to us. All crew members are currently healthy.

The children have asked for a kitten. If you can find a way, it would be most appreciated. This has been a very trying time.

Sai Dexter, COMMANDER
Expeditionary & Settlement Team
United States Territory, Mars

Chapter Twenty-Five

SITUATION REPORT

"Where's Albie?" Meems asked me when I came to supper.

"He said he's not hungry," I told her.

Concern flickered over her face. "Is he getting sick?"

I wasn't sure. Could you get sick from love?

"He's just listening to sad songs," I explained.

"I see," she said. "I'll take him a plate later."

"*Bonjour*," Flossy said as she sat down at the table. She was wearing a French scarf around her neck.

"*Quoi de neuf?*" Vera replied.

"What does that mean?" Meems asked curiously.

"'What's up?'" Vera explained.

"My favorite slang is *C'est top!*, which means 'That's great!'" Flossy said. "The French have lots of cute phrases!"

Salty Bill started ladling a thick stew into our bowls.

"*Merci!*" Flossy chirped.

I had a sudden thought. "We have to thank them!" I said.

"Thank who?" Trey asked.

"Everyone! We should send thank-you notes to the French and the other countries that helped us!" I said.

"I don't know," Sai began, just as Meems said, "What a lovely idea."

"You're always telling us we should send thank-you notes! We send them to people we've never even met! How can we possibly not send them to people we know?" Vera argued. "It's just good manners."

"They have a point," Eliana agreed.

Sai didn't look happy. "All right."

"*C'est top!*" Flossy said.

Everyone—grown-ups and kids—wrote thank-you notes. Albie's note to Layla looked more like a book. The next morning, Sai delivered them on the train to the various settlements.

I discovered the plastic box a few days later. I was on dust duty, and it had been left on the platform in the train tunnel. Inside were letters for everyone. Flossy shrieked when she saw her pile, and Albie smiled so big that I thought he would tip over. I got three letters—from Taavi and Wei and Amélie.

Bonjour, Bell,
How is Leo? I miss you. Tell Flossy the
baby is still stinky.
Mes amitiés,
Amélie

Even Sai got a letter: from Commander Laurent. He studied it for a long time.

"What did she say?" I asked him.

He cleared his throat. "Advice on technical issues," he said in a neutral voice. "Dust remediation and such."

"Sounds exciting," I said.

"Yes," he said.

⚛

Soon we were exchanging notes with the other settlements every few days.

Sometimes there were small gifts in the plastic box. A bottle of cinnamon. A soft knit hat. A pair of goggles with tinted lenses. A packet of seeds.

But it wasn't just the letters and treats that made the difference. It was the feeling that we weren't alone anymore. We had friends who cared about us. Our world was so much bigger now.

Taavi sent me drawings of cats, and Wei sent me funny

jokes. Amélie mostly sent me daily reports about the baby. She made a comic and called it *The Daily Baby*.

THE DAILY BABY

TODAY THE BABY POOPED!
EVERYONE CHEERED. THEN THE BABY SPIT UP.
IT WAS ANOTHER EXCITING DAY WITH THE BÉBÉ.

She never failed to make me laugh.

The biggest surprise came a few days later. Someone—we weren't sure who—sent us four Ping-Pong paddles and a small bag of balls. All we needed was a table.

Trey and I ambushed Darby and Eliana at breakfast.

"Can you make us a Ping-Pong table?" Trey asked.

"I'm not awake yet. Did you say 'Ping-Pong table'?" Eliana replied with a yawn.

"Here, Peanut Butter," Darby said, handing her a cup of coffee.

She took a gulp and blinked at us. "All right, what is all this about?"

"They sent us Ping-Pong paddles and balls!" I said.

"I see," Eliana said with a wry look. "Where will it go?"

"What about the recreation room?" Trey suggested.

"But that will take up a lot of space," Sai grumbled.

"The recreation room *is* supposed to be for fun," Darby pointed out.

"Please?" I asked.

Eliana looked at Sai. "Come on, Sai. What's the harm in it?"

"Fine," he huffed.

"Woo-hoo!" Trey said, and we bumped fists.

Everyone pitched in. Eliana helped us design it. Darby found a large piece of plastic that made a perfect tabletop. Meems knit a net of purple yarn. Sai even let us use some plastic barrels for the base. The result didn't look as nice as the French Ping-Pong table, but it worked, and that's all that mattered.

That evening after supper, we kids played Ping-Pong. We laughed and smiled and had fun. It was perfect. Only one thing was missing.

Our friends.

·❂·

I was sitting with Flossy and Vera in the recreation room, watching a French digi-reel. It had shown up that morning in the plastic box.

Albie walked into the room.

"I need your advice," he said to Vera and Flossy.

Vera waved her hand. "Speak."

"I want to make a gift for Layla," Albie said. "But I don't know what girls like."

"What about flowers?" Flossy suggested.

"We don't have any flowers here," Albie said.

"We could make some," Flossy said. "Algae-paper flowers?"

Albie brightened. "That's a good idea!"

Vera shook her head. "Why would she want paper flowers when they grow real ones in the French settlement?"

I was confused.

"Wait," I said. "I thought flowers were for friends."

"Flowers are romantic," Flossy said. "For when you're in love."

In love?

Did that mean Commander Laurent liked Sai?

Maybe even . . . loved him?

In the end, Flossy convinced Albie to make Layla some chocolate fudge. Apparently, it was also an Earth tradition to give candy when you were in love. That sounded like a good tradition to me.

"Do you think she'll like it?" Albie asked, staring at the perfectly wrapped package of fudge that he'd made.

It was after supper, and we were all in the mess hall. Salty Bill had served the extra fudge for dessert. It was a delicious treat. Too bad Sai was missing out on it. He was up in the COR working on something.

"It's candy," I told him.

"I'm sure she'll love it," Meems assured him.

"Remember the first present I gave you, Peanut Butter?" Darby asked Eliana with a smile.

"Did you give her candy, too?" Flossy asked him.

Eliana snorted. "I wish. He gave me a pair of boots."

"Boots?" Vera asked.

"She was complaining that her feet were cold," he said. "I asked a buddy who was coming to the lunar settlement from Earth to bring a pair of boots."

"Well, they were warm, I guess," Eliana said.

"You loved those boots, Peanut Butter," he teased her. She blushed.

Sai walked into the mess hall with an expression I couldn't decipher.

"I just heard from Command," he said.

"What did they have to say?" Meems asked.

"Are they sending a kitten?" I asked. "I have a name all picked out!"

"If they send a kitten, I want to choose the name this time!" Vera said.

"No way," Trey said. "You'll just pick some sad name and make the kitten wear all black."

Flossy snorted a laugh, and Vera glared at her.

"Here," Sai said, handing me his digi-slate. "Read for yourself."

I read it out loud.

[VIA SECURE COMMUNICATION]

DATE: 10.13.2091
FROM: US Terrestrial Command
TO: CDR Dexter
MESSAGE: Re: Situation Report

You do not have authorization to liaise with hostile
nations. Tensions remain high here. Cease all contact
immediately.
    Request for kitten denied.

> Evelyn Morris, COMMANDER
> Mars Space Command
> United States

No one said anything. It felt like all the air had been
sucked out of the room.

"Cease all contact?" Flossy whispered.

Vera exploded. "It's not fair!" she shouted.

I agreed. And the kitten part seemed kind of mean.

"Vera," Meems said.

"They didn't help us when we needed them the most!"
she shouted.

"It wasn't their fault. The launch window wasn't in our favor," Sai said. But there wasn't much conviction in his voice. It was like he was trying to convince himself.

"But why do we listen to them?" Vera demanded. "Why?"

"Because it's a direct order," Sai said.

"But my birthday's coming up!" Vera cried. "We were going to have a party and invite everyone!"

"You'll have other birthdays," Sai said.

"But I'll only turn sixteen once!"

Meems leaned forward. "We'll have a cake and—"

"I don't want a cake! I want my friends!" Vera shouted.

"I'm sorry," Sai said. "We have to listen to Command."

"It's dumb! They're all dumb! I hate them!" Vera shouted.

Albie looked miserable. He stared at the pretty package of candy.

"Not much point now, I guess," he said.

He walked over to the trash can and tossed the box in.

⚙

The next morning, Sai officially cut off contact with the other countries.

Chapter Twenty-Six

ALL IS NOT WELL

The dust storm had finally ended. The sky was clear for the first time in months.

But belowground, a different kind of storm was raging. A dark, gloomy sadness had fallen on the settlement. It crept around corners and curled up on the couch. It made mealtimes silent and stole away laughter. Everything felt diminished, bland, like all the color was gone.

It was in random quiet moments that I missed my friends the most. Like when I was brushing my teeth or petting Leo or doing nothing at all.

Like now. It was early morning and I was lying in bed. Instead of getting a few more minutes of sleep, I was thinking about Amélie. What would she do today? Would she and Taavi and Wei play Ping-Pong? What digi-reel would they watch tonight?

The breakfast chime sounded in the distance. Albie

didn't move in his bed. I knew he was awake because the room was quiet: no snoring.

"Isn't it time to get up?" I asked.

"I guess so," he said without enthusiasm.

Albie wasn't the same. Sure, he did his chores and went through the motions, but he never smiled now.

We arrived late at breakfast. Salty Bill brought out a tray of green buns for us.

"I made you kids a special treat," Salty Bill announced. "They're *all* chocolate!"

"Thanks," I said, taking one.

I took a bite of the chewy bun. It didn't taste as good as I remembered. Then again, nothing seemed as nice these days. Of course, I was happy to be home. But I'd glimpsed another kind of life, and it had been snatched away. It was like a digi-reel I would never get to finish.

Sai cleared his throat loudly. "So, Trey, how would you like to be my new junior apprentice?"

"No thank you," Trey said quietly.

"What?" Sai asked. "But you've always wanted to apprentice."

Trey wouldn't meet Sai's eyes. "I changed my mind."

I wasn't surprised. We had all lost our spark. There was nothing to look forward to anymore. No reason to be excited.

Take Flossy. She'd stopped dressing up in her fun Earth

outfits. Next to her, Vera was picking at her breakfast. Her hair was growing out, and her bangs were sloppy. They were distinctly un-Vera. Even the grown-ups noticed something was wrong.

"Are you going to cut your hair again, Vera?" Meems asked.

"What's the point? It's not like anyone will ever see it," she replied loudly.

Meems sighed.

"In fact, maybe I'll pierce my nose. I hear that's an Earth custom," Vera taunted. "Who cares what I look like, right?"

Vera knocked back her chair and stormed out of the mess hall.

"It'll be fine," Meems said, trying to sound positive. "She's just going through a phase."

"It won't be fine!" Flossy cried. "And she's not going through a phase!"

She leapt up and ran the same way.

I wanted to run away, too.

Because I finally understood how Muffin must have felt. This settlement—my home—didn't feel so cozy anymore. I felt trapped.

Like a mouse in a cage.

A few days later, Meems announced it was time to clean out Phinneus's bedroom. Trey and I volunteered to help Meems sort through his belongings. We would box them up to send to his nephew on Earth on the next supply ship.

While his office was messy, his bedroom was oddly tidy. Everything was in its place, right down to the way he folded his socks (in balls, like cat toys). His bed was still made, corners perfect, sheets tight. I pictured his head lying on the pillow, and my chest felt heavy.

Everywhere, there were reminders that his life had been cut short. A needle with thread next to a button. A book with a dog-eared page on the table next to his bed, waiting to be finished.

I picked up a digi-pic of Phinneus and his wife from the dresser. It was from their wedding. His wife was wearing a big, fluffy dress, and he was in a suit and looked young. He couldn't have been much older than Albie.

"That was a lovely dress," Meems said.

We got down to work, sorting papers, clothes, books, and other things.

"What about these?" Trey asked Meems, holding up a book titled *The Astrobiologists' Almanac.*

"Anything that's research- or Mars-based stays here," she said.

He put the book in the Stay pile and kept going.

While Trey and Meems went through Phinneus's closet, I unpacked his dresser. There wasn't much worth sending to Earth—it was mostly clothes. There was a T-shirt that said "Mars's First Farmer: I'm Raising Dust."

Deep in the back of his sock drawer, I found something unexpected—a notebook. I flipped through the first few pages. It looked like a scientific diary, about the weather and different seed tests.

Then I saw this notation:

> What a wonderful day! Bell has arrived in our settlement.
> We love him already.

My heart tripped.

"Meems," I said, "can I keep this?"

"What is it?" she asked.

I showed her the page.

She read it and looked at me.

"Of course you can keep it," she said, and smiled. "After all, you were his family, too."

That night, I settled down under my cozy quilt, with Leo asleep on top by my feet, and read Phinneus's diary.

Reading Phinneus's words made me feel like he was in the room with me. I could hear his voice in every line. He had such a funny sense of humor.

Broccoli harvest successful!

A week later, he wrote:

Broccoli banned from menu. Commander Sai says everyone is gassy.
(Yours truly included.)

Other observations about life on Mars were sprinkled among his scientific notes, which mostly focused on hydration levels, the moons, test samples of algae paper. There was a tiny folded note that said "I'm sorry" with no signature. Adorable doodles of the cats in the margins.

I could feel his excitement and worry in every word. So much was riding on him. There would be no survival without food.

This is such a heavy responsibility.

He worked so hard. Harder than I'd ever imagined. Sometimes he got up in the middle of the night to make sure everything was working properly. His handwriting was neat and easy to read, although it became loopy when he was excited about something.

MARS HOURS	CROP	STATUS
18:25	Lettuces	Sufficient water
24:15	Lettuces	Leak—clog?
24:30	Lettuces	Leak mitigated
03:15	Lettuces	AIW

It took me a while to understand his shorthand. But when I did, it made so much sense. "AIW" was short for "All is well."

Halfway through, the diary changed: fewer scientific notations and more observations about people.

Meems received news that her first grandchild was born, and she cried all day.
She will never hold him.

Another time, he wrote:

Today is Rose's birthday.
Happy birthday, sweetheart.
Wait for me.

Two dozen pages later, he started writing about the "Terrible Tragedy."

> We buried Lissa today.
> Mars weeps.

And a few pages later, he wrote:

> There is no reasoning with Sai over this tragedy. He is blind to everything but his own grief and listens to Command.

Months passed before he started writing again.

> Nothing is the same. I miss our friends dearly. We are so terribly alone now. The children are the only thing that keeps us going. Their happy smiles are a reprieve from our loneliness.

This must have been when they cut off communication with the other settlements. But some passages made me wonder.

> It makes no sense to me. Petyr adored Lissa. He would never have left her without a reason. And Commander Laurent has an

*unshakable character. I do not believe what
they say. There is more to this story.*

Then the diary ended.

·Ö·

The next morning was laundry day. I went to Meems's room. She beamed at me when she opened her door.

"I'll do your sheets," I told her.

"You're such a good boy," she said.

I really wasn't good; I had questions.

After the dirty sheets were in a bundle by the door, I worked up my courage.

"I'm confused," I told her.

"About what, Kitten?" she asked.

"Lissa," I said. "I read Phinneus's diary. Who was Petyr?"

"I haven't heard that name in a long time," she said. "He's Russian. A geologist. Phinneus was very fond of him."

"What does he have to do with Lissa's death?"

Meems sighed heavily. "I should have expected this."

"Why did they leave Lissa behind?"

She smiled sadly. "I have no idea. Only Commander Laurent and Petyr know what happened, and we have never spoken to them about it."

"What?"

"You have to understand, it was a very difficult time," she said. "There was talk of war on Earth. Sides were being chosen over Antarctica. Sai was under incredible pressure. Command ordered us to cease all contact with the other countries. But he ignored it for a time. After all, we were literally worlds away. We continued on as we had from the beginning. We traded and socialized and conducted joint missions."

She looked down at her hands. They looked so wrinkled suddenly.

"Commander Laurent was out in a rover with Lissa and Petyr, collecting samples," she continued. "An alert went out, saying their rover had gone missing. You know the rest. Sai and Eliana found Lissa. She died from her injuries."

"Why didn't you try to find out what happened?"

"Sai suspended all communications with the other countries," she said simply. "We tried to reason with him, but he was inconsolable. Lissa was his best friend's daughter. He'd grown up with her father, Will. Sai had promised to take care of Lissa on Mars. He'd loved her like she was his own daughter. After Lissa died and he contacted her parents, he didn't leave his room for days."

"So you still don't know what happened?"

She shook her head.

"No," she said. "And I suppose we never will."

I finally understood what Phinneus had tried to tell me about weeds. Our settlement was overgrown with bad feelings—weeds—from long ago.

And they were strangling us to death.

DATE: 10.28.2091
FROM: CDR Dexter
TO: US Terrestrial Command
MESSAGE: Situation Report

Morale is low.
Please advise.

Sai Dexter, COMMANDER
Expeditionary & Settlement Team
United States Territory, Mars

Chapter Twenty-Seven
PLEASE HELP

I dragged through my after-supper chores. I was exhausted; I hadn't gotten a good night's sleep in days, and it wasn't due to Albie's snoring. He had finally moved into Phinneus's old room, and Trey was back with me. It was because every time I tried to fall asleep, my mind raced. I couldn't stop thinking about Lissa, Commander Laurent, Petyr, and Sai. It was like a puzzle with a missing piece. I knew what the outline looked like, but the middle was confusing.

I yawned as I did my rounds. I was on dust duty, and Leo trailed after me. We'd discovered how he'd gotten to the French settlement: there was a hole in an air duct that connected to the train tunnel. Sai had sealed it up tight, so now Leo was stuck here, just like us. I think he was sad about not getting any more tasty treats.

The corridors were quiet. I missed the noise of the

French settlement most of all. Someone was always talking or laughing or arguing. I even missed the sound of the
baby crying.

As usual, my last stop was the train tunnel. I had just
emptied the dust when I saw a folded note taped to the
outside of the door. It hadn't been there yesterday evening
when I'd done my rounds, so someone must have placed it
there early this morning.

I unfolded it and scanned the words quickly.

> *Bell,*
> *   Please help us! Come tomorrow. It's*
> *urgent!*
>
> *   —Amélie*

My bucket fell to the ground, forgotten, as I ran.

All the kids huddled around my bed, looking at the note.

"What did Sai say when you showed it to him?" Flossy
asked me.

"He thought I wrote it," I said. "That I was trying to
trick him into letting us visit the French settlement."

"You?" Vera scoffed. "If anyone would write a note like
this, it would be me."

"Where did you find it?" Trey asked.

"In the train tunnel. It was taped to the back of the door," I said.

Vera flopped down on my bed. "Well, what are we going to do?"

"What can we do?" Flossy asked. "Sai doesn't even believe Amélie wrote the note. Which, by the way, he should. I've seen Bell's handwriting."

"It's not that bad," I protested.

Albie looked worried. "What do you think's going on at the French settlement? What if they're sick? What about Layla?"

"Why don't *you* talk to Sai, Flossy?" Trey suggested. "He'll listen to you."

It was a good idea. Sai respected Flossy.

"Right," she said, nodding. "I'll go find him."

We didn't have to wait long. She was back less than five minutes later.

"Well?" Vera asked.

She shook her head. "Sai said no. He said even if Bell didn't make it up, it was probably one of the other French kids, playing a prank."

"But they wouldn't do that!" I insisted.

It didn't matter. Sai's mind was already made up.

·❀·

The next morning on my dust rounds, I lingered in the algae farm. I saw traces of Phinneus everywhere: in the wall charts noting the water's pH balance, in the cookie jar on his desk, in the container of Earth soil.

My eyes landed on Phinneus's ratty blue sweater, hanging on the back of his chair. I picked it up and hugged it tight. It still smelled like him—like Earth soil and algae. Memories of Phinneus flooded out. His endless curiosity. The way his eyes brightened when he talked about plants. How he made funny voices for characters when he read to me.

Commander Laurent was right. Good memories were important. They kept us going. But the grown-ups had forgotten that. They couldn't remember what life was like before everything went wrong. They needed someone to remind them.

Someone like me.

·☼·

It was lunchtime, and we were sitting at a table. Salty Bill ladled stew into my bowl.

"I had the best bread in the French settlement," I told him.

His head snapped up. "A baguette?"

"You were right! It was so good," I said.

"I told you."

"Remember that amazing dessert they made?" Meems mused. "It was custard with dried cherries in a piecrust. I dream about that dessert sometimes."

"Did they have parties back then?" I asked.

"There were wonderful parties!" Eliana said.

"The Halloween party was one for the ages," Darby said.

"I seem to recall Sai dancing," Meems said with a mischievous smile.

Sai frowned. "I'm sure I didn't."

"Tell me more stories," I prompted them.

And that's all I needed to do.

Meems and Eliana and Darby and Salty Bill couldn't stop reminiscing about friends, fun, and food. They talked about silly pranks they played and adventures they had. Sai's expression got stonier and stonier.

I took a deep breath and said, "Are we going to help them?"

"Help who?" Salty Bill asked.

"The French settlement. They're in trouble."

"What kind of trouble?" Darby asked.

I pulled out the note. "They left us this."

Sai shook his head. "The children made that up—"

"Let me see it," Eliana demanded.

I handed it to her. She read it and passed it to Darby.

"Where did you find this?" she asked.

"It was in the train tunnel," I said.

Meems had the note now. She scanned it and looked at Sai.

"Really, Sai," she said, sounding like a disappointed parent.

"Bell wrote that," Sai said.

"You think I don't know my Bell's handwriting?" she countered.

His looked down quickly, as if embarrassed.

"Did you know that lions without a pride don't live long?" I asked.

"What?" Sai asked.

"We're like lions," I explained. "We're alone on Mars. We need the people in the other settlements to survive. We need a pride."

"Bell's right," Meems said. "This has gone on long enough, Sai. They saved us. Now it's our turn."

"But Command—" he protested.

Eliana got up and walked to the door.

"Where are you going?" Sai asked.

"To make sure the train is charged," she said.

"Right behind you, Peanut Butter," Darby said, following his wife.

"I'll get my med kit," Meems called.

I flushed with happiness.

"Wait!" Sai shouted. "We're not going anywhere!"

Everyone froze.

Then Salty Bill stood up and crossed his arms. "Commander, I'm not cooking another meal until we go to the French settlement and check on them. Understood?"

Sai's shoulders drooped.

"Copy that," he said.

Not that Sai ever had a choice. Like he always said, the most important person really was the cook.

❀

"I can't believe we're back here," Trey whispered to me as we sat next to each other in the train.

"At least we're not alone this time," I said with a grin.

Everyone was packed into Percy with us. Sai had radioed ahead to tell them we were all coming. And we weren't going empty-handed. There were boxes of emergency supplies, like glow sticks, food, water, and bandages. Salty Bill even brought a pie he had baked the day before.

When we arrived at the French settlement, Layla answered the door. Her face was pale and she was wearing Albie's ball cap.

"Albie!" she cried, throwing herself into his arms. "We'd almost lost hope!"

Albie hugged her tight. "What's wrong? What happened?"

"I'll show you! Quickly!" she urged, pulling him down the hallway, walking fast.

The rest of us followed them until finally we were standing outside the recreation room.

"In here," Layla said, and slipped through the door.

We quickly filed into the dark room after her.

"Where's the emergen—" Sai said. But before he could finish his sentence, the lights suddenly flicked on to reveal a room full of people. A huge sign that said HAPPY BIRTHDAY, VERA! was strung from the ceiling, and there was a birthday cake.

"Surprise!" everyone shouted.

Vera's stunned expression proved it was actually possible to keep a secret on Mars.

"Bell!" Amélie shouted, running over to me.

"Amélie," I cried as we hugged.

"So this was all a trick to get us to come here?" Sai asked.

Amélie rolled her eyes at him. "It wasn't a trick. We needed your help. You can't have a surprise party without the birthday girl!"

Meems snorted a laugh.

Sai turned and glared at her.

It was wonderful to catch up with all my friends, although Captain Laurent wasn't there. She had gone to the Chinese settlement to help with something.

At first, it seemed like two different parties: the kids on one side of the room and the grown-ups on the other. While we chatted and laughed, the grown-ups stood around awkwardly.

But after the cake and presents, the teens turned up the music and started dancing. That's when the party really got going. Seeing all the kids dancing seemed to melt the invisible ice. The next thing I knew, Salty Bill was slapping the French chef on the back and Meems was hugging an older woman. Eliana and Darby chatted with some grown-ups from the Chinese settlement; they'd worked together on the lunar colony. It was like a reunion. Everyone was happy.

Except for Sai.

He sat stiffly on the side of the room, back rigid, as if he wished he was anywhere but there.

Chapter Twenty-Eight
MARS WEEPS

Soft yellow light bled from the fake window on our bed-room wall. It was morning and the room was quiet. With Trey in the bed across from mine, there was no snoring. I could actually hear when Leo padded across the floor now.

I stared up at our map spanning the wall. In our imag-inings, we had forgotten the most important thing for a successful world: other people. All the beautiful buildings and rovers and monorails weren't much good if you didn't have anyone to share them with.

The morning bell chimed in the distance. It was time to get up. But Trey just pulled the pillow over his head. He was probably still tired—he'd gotten home late from the Chinese settlement, where the older teenagers had had a digi-reel marathon of Earth musicals.

"Time to get up," I said.

He groaned. "Ugh."

"It's rover day!"

"Oh yeah," he said, and jumped out of bed.

Today Eliana was teaching us—and kids from any of the other settlements who were interested—some of the basics of fixing a rover. She'd said that since we were so good at breaking rovers, we might as well learn how to repair them.

Life was different since Vera's surprise birthday party. We went back and forth to the other settlements for everything from playing Ping-Pong to borrowing a spare part to taking lessons. Flossy and Vera joined kids at the French settlement in the afternoon to learn French. Albie rotated around the settlements, eager to learn different styles of cooking. Trey had begun apprenticing with someone from the Russian settlement. As for me, I was learning Finnish.

The mess hall was bustling when Trey and I walked in for breakfast. We grabbed our plates and stood in line.

"What's for breakfast?" I asked Salty Bill.

"Scrambled eggs and toast," he said, and I swear he almost smiled.

Eggs were another bonus. The Chinese delivered a basket to any settlement that wanted them.

Trey and I sat down with our plates and dug in.

"Bell," Meems said, "can you take a plate of food to Sai? I don't think he's had breakfast."

"Sure," I said.

This was another thing that had changed since the birthday party. Sai was always in his workroom during meals these days. He claimed to be busy fixing things, but I was starting to wonder if *he* was what was broken. Vera said that the grown-ups had taken a vote about whether to continue to see the other settlements. Everyone had voted yes except for Sai.

I made up a plate of food and headed to his workshop. He was sitting at his desk, staring at the 3D printer.

"I brought you breakfast," I said, handing him the plate.

"Thank you," he said, but he didn't move to eat the food. He just stared at it.

"Don't you like scrambled eggs?" I asked him.

He looked at me. "I love them."

"What are you working on?" I asked him.

"A part for the new printer," he said. "I've tried again and again, but I can't seem to get it right."

"Why don't you ask if any of the other settlements have one?"

He shook his head. "It's not a good idea to rely on others."

"How come?"

Sai looked at me. "Because they'll just disappoint you."

Eliana's rover lesson was a big hit. Afterward, Salty Bill put out cookies in the mess hall for us.

I sat with Amélie and nibbled on a cookie.

"Commander Laurent said we can have a sleepover," she told me. "Taavi and Wei are coming."

"What's that?" I asked.

"It's when you get to stay at my settlement overnight, and we watch digi-reels and eat popcorn."

That sounded fun to me.

"What if we have the sleepover here?" I asked Amélie.

"Here?"

"I've already stayed at your settlement, but you've never stayed at mine!" Leo brushed up against my leg. "And we have Leo!"

"Taavi will love that," Amélie said.

"I'll ask Meems!" I said.

·⚙·

Meems agreed that I could have the other kids sleep over, although she did mutter something under her breath about how no one would actually be getting any sleep.

So a few days later, I waited by the door to the train tunnel for my guests. Amélie was the first to arrive. Commander Laurent had brought her, and someone else as well: a man with dark, sad eyes.

"Bonjour!" I said to them.

Commander Laurent smiled at me. "*Bonjour,* Bell. Are you excited for your sleepover?"

"*Oui!*" I said.

"Before I go, I need to speak to Meems."

"Sure," I said.

Everyone followed me to the mess hall. Meems was sitting at the table with a cup of tea. When she saw us, she gasped.

"Sylvie!" she said. "And Petyr!"

This was Petyr? The one who was with Lissa during the accident?

Meems rushed over to Commander Laurent, and they clasped hands.

"Why, Sylvie, you look exactly the same," Meems told her with a smile.

Commander Laurent laughed, a light, happy sound. "Your eyes must be failing, because I am quite certain I did not have all this gray hair the last time you saw me."

Then Meems walked over to Petyr. "How have you been?" she asked him.

"As well as can be expected living underground on a freezing-cold planet," he said.

"The same old sense of humor, I see," she teased.

"Meems," Commander Laurent said. "We'd like to talk to Sai."

"Good luck," Meems said. "He's in his workroom."

"I remember the way well," Commander Laurent said.

After the two of them left the mess hall, Meems shook her head. "That was enough excitement for me. Have a fun sleepover."

Then she was gone.

"I can't believe that just happened," I said.

"What?" Amélie asked.

"That man! That's Petyr!"

She lifted a shoulder. "I know."

"Oh, just come on!" I told her, and grabbed her hand and ran down the corridor.

We slowed when we heard raised voices. I put a finger to my lips, and Amélie nodded. We peeked out from around a corner and could see Commander Laurent and Petyr talking to Sai.

"How could you leave her, Petyr?" Sai asked.

"You don't understand, Sai!" Commander Laurent said.

"Commander Laurent was badly injured," Petyr said. "I had to get her help! She was bleeding heavily from her head and was unconscious."

"But what about Lissa?" Sai asked in an agonized voice. "She was hurt, too!"

"Her leg was broken," Petyr said, "but Lissa assured me she could wait. I could only carry one person. We both knew that Commander Laurent didn't have much time. I would return for Lissa."

"But you didn't go back," Sai said.

"Because I ran out of oxygen and fainted just outside

the French settlement," Petyr explained. "Luckily, Armand was in the communications room and saw me fall with Commander Laurent."

Sai shook his head. "I didn't know any of this."

"I sent many transmissions explaining the situation afterward," Commander Laurent said gently.

Sai looked ashamed. "I never opened them. I deleted them all."

"But why? I don't understand, Sai."

"We received the alert about the rover being lost," Sai said. "When we found it, Lissa was the only one there. I—I thought you'd left her there to die."

"How could you believe such a thing?" Commander Laurent asked, shocked.

Sai looked miserable. "I don't know."

"How did she die?" Petyr asked anxiously. "I couldn't believe it when I heard! She'd only had a broken leg."

"Meems suspects it was a blood clot from the broken leg," Sai said.

"I was going to go back for her, I swear!" Petyr said.

"It wasn't your fault, Petyr," Sai said in a pained voice. "I'm so sorry for thinking the worst. Please forgive me."

"Forgive you?" Petyr asked. "I was the one who wasn't strong enough to save her!"

Sai shook his head. "Neither of us could have saved her. But I was the one who let my grief and anger tear apart everything we'd built together."

Petyr looked stunned.

Sai gave him a quick, hard hug.

"Thank you for looking after Lissa when I couldn't," he said in a husky voice.

Petyr nodded. "I'll meet you back at the train," he said to Commander Laurent.

Then he turned and walked along the corridor toward us. I pulled Amélie down behind a stack of plastic boxes.

Now it was just Sai and Commander Laurent.

"If I'd been conscious, Sai, I would have made him take her," Commander Laurent told him.

Sai gently traced the jagged scar on her forehead.

"All these years, and I didn't even know you'd been hurt. Can you ever forgive me?" Sai asked brokenly.

"There's nothing to forgive," she said.

He held her hand to his cheek. "My sweet Larry. I've missed you so much."

Larry? This was *Larry?*

"I've missed you, too, Sai," Commander Laurent said.

Then Sai leaned in and kissed her.

And kept kissing her.

Amélie's mouth fell open in shock.

Mine did, too.

"Bisou bisou," Amélie whispered, making a face.

Honestly, grown-ups were worse than teenagers.

Chapter Twenty-Nine

PRIDE

It was a beautiful morning. The sky was pink as far as the eye could see, the red surface welcoming. Mars was radiant like a smile.

This day had been planned for a while. We put on our environmental suits and went to the graveyard. Commander Laurent and Petyr placed bouquets of flowers on the graves of Lissa and Phinneus. I knew Phinneus would have liked it.

After that, we piled into rovers and headed to the French settlement. It was the site of the first-ever Mars Ping-Pong Tournament. It had been my and Amélie's idea.

As we drove along in the *Yellow Submarine*, Commander Laurent pointed to an enormous crater in the ground.

"That's where the meteorite struck," she said.

Trey looked at me with an excited expression on his face.

"Can we see it?" Trey asked.

"Please?" I asked.

"I suppose so," Sai said.

Eliana parked the rover, and we all got out to look. The crater was enormous.

"It's got to be over eighteen meters wide," Albie said with a low whistle.

"Too bad it wasn't an alien ship," Trey said.

"Maybe they'll come next time," Amélie said, and grinned at me. "They can eat the poopy baby."

The meteorite—just a rock—wasn't very large. It was probably only a few centimeters bigger than me.

"How could a rock that size make such a big crater?" I asked.

Sai looked down at me.

"Something doesn't need to be big to have an impact," he said, and smiled. "Kind of like you."

☼

The recreation room of the French settlement was packed with Ping-Pong tables. Kids from every country had been invited. There was food and music and laughter. It was perfect.

Then we started playing. It was even fun to watch.

Taavi had a way of adding spin to the ball that gave him fast shots.

After a while, Amélie challenged the adults to a round.

"Grown-ups versus kids," she proposed with a sly look.

"I don't think . . . ," Sai began.

"Come on, Commander," Commander Laurent said, and looped her arm through his. "Let's show them what we've got."

Sai and Commander Laurent were a pretty good team. But not as good as me and Amélie. Kids are just better at some things. Like knowing that friends are important.

We played game after game of Ping-Pong, to the cheers of the whole planet. It didn't matter what the score was in the end. Because we had all won.

We were the pride of Mars.

AUTHOR'S NOTE

Though this book was written before Covid-19, the copy-editing and final production happened during the pandemic. I could never have imagined how eerily relevant and poignant this fictional virus on Mars would become.

The inspiration for this futuristic book actually came from the past, though. My father was raised on a dairy farm during the Great Depression. Even though it was a terrible time—for both his family and the country—neighbors pitched in and helped one another. After my father grew up, he became a fighter pilot and served in the Korean War, and eventually he became a pediatrician. (He was no slouch!)

My flyboy father is in his flight suit. (I still have the helmet.)

After he passed away, I was eager to learn more about him. I had always been interested in space. So I was excited to learn that many of the early astronauts, including Buzz Aldrin, Neil Armstrong, and John Glenn, had been pilots in the Korean War, too. They were just like my dad. It made the idea of going to space seem possible to me.

So I began to wonder: What would it would be like to grow up on Mars? Not a high-tech terraformed Mars, but a small, family farm version. What would daily life be like? Where would you play? What would you eat? Would there be chores? Who would be your neighbors? Most of all, what would a child growing up on Mars think of Earth—a place they had never visited but only heard about? Then I imagined Bell: a curious, cat-loving, big-hearted eleven-year-old living on the Red Planet. And I was off and running.

Many of the things mentioned in this book are grounded in science. Using underground lava tubes—the large tunnel-like spaces left behind by flowing lava—has been proposed by scientists and engineers. The tubes could prove to be a practical habitat that would provide a natural barrier for humans from radiation, dust, and freezing temperatures.

Global dust storms on Mars are indeed a big deal. Occurring every few years, they can block light from the sun and last for weeks. During the global dust storm of 2018,

NASA's solar-powered rover *Opportunity* went offline per-manently.

Artist's rendering of NASA Mars Exploration Rover on the surface of Mars

As in the book, traveling to Mars has always been a complicated matter. Mars's orbit brings the planet closest to Earth once every twenty-six months. This is known as a Mars close approach and is the reason that missions to Mars are timed to take advantage of this situation.

Both NASA and the European Space Agency have suggested algae (specifically, spirulina) as a food source. Algae could also potentially supply oxygen. An algae-powered bioreactor that converts carbon dioxide to oxygen has been tested on the International Space Station.

Finally, the enduring friendship of America and France has always been an inspiration to me. I think there's a little bit of Lafayette in Bell.

"No obstacle, no disappointment, no sorrow distracts me from the unique goal of my life, the well-being of all and freedom everywhere."
—Marquis de Lafayette, beloved "son" of America

The dream of humans going to Mars has been kept alive by countless people, from astronauts to scientists to entrepreneurs. I firmly believe we will overcome the many obstacles to a journey to the Red Planet. But what happens when we finally get there will prove far more difficult than the technical challenges. It's my hope that a future Mars will be a place where neighbors help one another and play Ping-Pong together. Ultimately, what this society looks like will depend on all of us.

(And maybe even the cats.)

My first visit to SpaceX in California

ADDITIONAL RESOURCES
TO CONTINUE THE CONVERSATION

WEBSITES

All About Algae
allaboutalgae.com/algae-basics

The Mars Society
marssociety.org

NASA Mars Exploration Program
mars.nasa.gov

BOOKS

Aldrin, Buzz, and Marianne Dyson. *Welcome to Mars: Making a Home on the Red Planet.* New York: National Geographic Children's Books, 2015.

Turner, Pamela S. *Life on Earth—and Beyond: An Astrobiologist's Quest.* Watertown, MA: Charlesbridge, 2008.

Zubrin, Robert. *The Case for Mars: The Plan to Settle the Red Planet and Why We Must.* New York: Free Press, 2011.

ACKNOWLEDGMENTS

I am so grateful to have had such generous assistance on my journey to the Red Planet. Special thanks to Dr. Chris McKay, Margarita Marinova, and Dr. Mary Beth Wilhelm. The Mars Society has been welcoming and incredibly helpful. I am especially indebted to Mario Colorado for his work on microalgae and Douglas D. Shull for his advice on lava tubes. Many thanks to Dr. Kjell Lindgren, Dr. Vincent Michaud, Dr. Dean Olson, Dr. Jeff Siegel, and Theresa Rogers for medical advice. In addition, thank you to the creative Rachel Hart for visual wizardry.

I have dear friends who helped me along the way, including Shannon Rosa, Craig Rosa, and Pamela Turner. My patient editor, Michelle Nagler, and my wonderful agent, Jill Grinberg, helped keep this ship on course!

Most of all, warm thanks to my dear friend and high school French teacher, Diane Cusumano.

Finally, a universal debt is owed to Dr. Robert Zubrin for keeping the dream of Mars alive.

Mars or bust!